BETWEEN TWO WORLDS

Hugo paused in order to fin— father has a job, in a school, to teach Latin and Greek. He is very keen for this job. When do you think—?"

"He'd be able to work?" Dr. Andrew sighed. "I'm afraid there's not much chance to him ever being able to do that, lad."

"Never?"

"You'll have to face the fact that he's going to be a semi-invalid. It was a massive heart attack, and he's lucky to be alive. It was sheer determination that pulled him through, if you ask me. But he's not going to be fit enough to do a full-time job ever again."

"This book draws on the same themes of family solidarity and strength of the human spirit that made the Petersons such a memorable family [in *Tug of War*]."
—*Voice of Youth Advocates*

"Evidence of their recovery from the trauma of war will please devotees of Lingard and her fictional clan."
—*Publishers Weekly*

BETWEEN TWO WORLDS

Joan Lingard

PUFFIN BOOKS

Acknowledgments

I would like to thank the following
for their helpful advice and comment:
David Kilgour, Bruce Hunter, Margaret Mackay,
and the Birkhans family.

PUFFIN BOOKS
Published by the Penguin Group
Penguin Books USA Inc., 375 Hudson Street, New York, New York 10014, U.S.A.
Penguin Books Ltd, 27 Wrights Lane, London W8 5TZ, England
Penguin Books Australia Ltd, Ringwood, Victoria, Australia
Penguin Books Canada Ltd, 10 Alcorn Avenue, Toronto, Ontario, Canada M4V 3B2
Penguin Books (N.Z.) Ltd, 182–190 Wairau Road, Auckland 10, New Zealand

Penguin Books Ltd, Registered Offices: Harmondsworth, Middlesex, England

First published in Great Britain by Hamish Hamilton Ltd. 1991
First published in the United States of America by Lodestar Books, an
affiliate of Dutton Children's Books, a division of Penguin Books USA Inc., 1991
Published in Puffin Books, 1993

1 3 5 7 9 10 8 6 4 2

LIBRARY OF CONGRESS CATALOGING-IN-PUBLICATION DATA
Lingard, Joan.
Between two worlds / Joan Lingard.   p. cm.
Summary: Arriving in their new homeland, Canada, after World War II,
a family of Latvian refugees is beset by serious illness and
financial hardship, and the three children must go out and find
jobs. Sequel to "Tug of war."
ISBN 0-14-036505-2
[1. Emigration and immigration—Fiction.   2. Refugees—Fiction.
3. Canada—Fiction.]   I. Title.
PZ7.L6626Be   1993   [Fic]—dc20   92-44006   CIP   AC

Printed in the United States of America
Set in Meridien

for Margaret Mackay
and Bruce Hunter

ONE

THE TIME is November, 1948; the place is Union Station, Toronto, Canada. There is a stir on the platform. A train, packed with immigrants from Europe, has come in from Quebec City, and a man has collapsed. He is lying in a crumpled heap, and a group of his fellow passengers have formed a ring around him, sheltering him from the wind. Kneeling by his side are a middle-aged woman, a boy of about twelve years, and an older boy and girl.

"Lukas," the woman says, gently turning his head to one side. The onlookers catch their breath. The man's face is a terrible purple, and his lips are a ghastly blue.

"We must get help for Father," the girl cries, jumping up. She holds out her hand to the older boy. "*Quickly, Hugo!*"

The Petersons family had arrived by ship in Quebec City the day before. The ten-day Atlantic crossing from Cuxhaven in Germany had been stormy. Most of the passengers had been ill, especially those who, like the

Petersons, had been bunked down on the lowest deck, where they'd felt every dip and swell. Their passage up the wide St. Lawrence river had been smoother, but even so, they had been impatient to feel land under their feet again.

Alien land. They would be strangers here. But they were used to that.

A bump, and the liner had docked. Sailors called instructions in two languages, French and English. Many of the travelers could understand neither. The moorings were secured, the gangway lowered. Excitement rippled like a small wave through those waiting to disembark as people began to shuffle forward.

"Keep together, now!" Lukas Petersons told his family.

He led the way, listing to the right as he walked, dragging his bad leg. The damp sea air had not been good for his old wound. He'd been shot in that leg when he'd been on the run from the Cheka—the Soviet secret police—during World War II. He'd been on their wanted list, on account of being a scholar and university professor.

Close behind Lukas came Kristina, then Tomas, the youngest in the family, and finally Astra and Hugo, who were twins and, at eighteen, six years Tomas's senior. Lukas had spoken in their own language, Latvian. Their fellow travelers spoke in many different tongues—Polish, Czech, Hungarian, Russian, Estonian, Lithuanian, and German. All were people displaced by war, come from Europe to settle in this new country.

"Did you hear that?" Astra turned to grin at Hugo, who gave her a light punch on the arm. *"Keep together!"*

Four years before, in 1944, when they had been fleeing from Latvia in the wake of the advancing Soviet Army, Hugo had been separated from the rest of his family. It had happened in the Polish port of Gdynia. He'd had his glasses knocked off, and when he'd bent

2

over to pick them up, he'd been kicked in the head and had fallen down unconscious. He still carried the scar on his forehead. He had found his family again in Hamburg, only days before setting sail for Canada.

"Don't worry! I'll stick like glue!"

But, although he made a joke of it, he could feel beads of perspiration starting around his hairline. He put up his arm to wipe them away. He'd always hated crowds, but after Gdynia, he found that he could scarcely breathe when caught up in the midst of one. The ten long days on the crowded boat had been difficult.

There would not be much chance of being separated here, however. The war was long over; there were no air raid sirens wailing, putting the fear of death into you, no planes screeching overhead or bombs exploding and people screaming. There was no threat of panic as there had been in Gdynia, no rush to get on trains to avoid being left behind. Everything here was organized and orderly.

One by one, struggling with suitcases and bags, they began to descend the gangway. On their chests were pinned labels giving their names and the names of their sponsors. In their hands they held the precious landing cards that would entitle them to become landed immigrants in Canada.

Tomas, following hard on the heels of his mother, almost bumped into her in his eagerness to get onto Canadian soil. He felt the gangway shift and sway beneath him. He smelled the smell of the docks: a mixture of rope and tar and the sea itself. Gulls swooped and cried, making more noise than the people.

And then he took the last step down, into Canada. He almost expected to feel an electric shock. He'd arrived! They had talked so much about North America that it was hard to believe they were actually here. He'd been a bit disappointed coming up the St. Lawrence; it had been so flat and colorless, somehow. It had rained, gray, November rain. He'd expected snow, deep, crisp, and even; and huge, towering forests so thick that if you went into them, you might be lost forever. There would be forests like that in some parts of Canada, his father said, but not in Toronto, where they were going. It was a city of some seven hundred thousand people. That sounded like an awful lot of people to Tomas. In Latvia they had lived in the country, and after the war, in southern Germany, in the small medieval town of Esslingen.

They crossed the dock and filed into a long wooden shed. "Customs and Immigration," said Astra. Everyone's papers had to be checked to see that they were in order. More standing in line, more waiting. Each person breathed easier as his or landing card was stamped.

Tomas had been allowed to carry his own card. He handed it over.

"So, you are from Latvia." The official brought his stamp down. He looked up at Tomas and smiled. "Welcome to Canada!"

"Thank you," said Tomas haltingly, trying out his English. He knew only a few words, unlike his father and Astra who were almost fluent. They were the ones in the family with an ear for languages. He'd meant to get down to learning English on the boat but had been too busy playing cards and Ping-Pong with some Ukrainian and Czech boys whom he'd met—when he'd not been sick.

As they came out of the Immigration shed, they were met by people handing out presents. After four years of being refugees, they were used to this. Whenever they had arrived at a new camp, they had been given something: leather belts, chocolate, tins of Spam. Once, it had been shaving brushes. Everyone, male and female, adult or child, had been given half a dozen.

4

Today the welcome gift consisted of a packet of tobacco, one of cigarette papers, and five dollars.

"Thank you," said Tomas again.

" 'Black Cat' tobacco." Astra read aloud from the label. "And 'Viscount' cigarette papers." She hooted with laughter. "Imagine!"

"They must think we all smoke," said Hugo.

"Maybe Canadian children do?" said Tomas.

"I would doubt it," his father answered firmly.

Astra said they could give their tobacco to him. "It will be better than some of that smelly stuff you put in your pipe!"

"I'm not sure that we should encourage him!" Kristina smiled and shook her head. She had been trying to persuade Lukas, though not too hard, to give up his pipe. She thought that he might be able to stop once they were settled. To be settled and not to have to move again! Would that be possible? It was what Lukas needed.

He had a cough, and his color was not good. None of that was surprising, considering how stressful the last four years of their lives had been. They'd been exiles, homeless, unable to return to their own country, leaving relatives and friends behind, the fate of some not even known. Latvia, along with the two other Baltic states of Estonia and Lithuania, had been taken over by the Soviet Union. The refugees had been shunted around Europe in trains, had lived in camps, often in appalling conditions, short of food and heat.

Kristina tried not to let Lukas see her watching him. He hated to be fussed over.

"We could sell the tobacco," Tomas suggested. "Or exchange it for chocolate. Or food," he added quickly, so as not to seem to be thinking too much of himself.

"We won't be selling and exchanging things here, Tomas," said his father. "This is North America! People don't go around selling to one another. There will be plenty of goods in the shops."

In Germany they had lived largely by barter and trading on the black market. It had been the only way to stay alive.

"Come on," urged Kristina. "We mustn't dawdle. We don't want to get left behind."

A train was waiting.

"Is this it?" Tomas was disappointed.

It was not a sleek, modern-looking train like some they'd seen in American magazines. These carriages were wooden and high-sided. Lukas thought that they might have been used to transport skiers and their equipment, or something of that nature. But there were seats for everyone, unlike the refugee trains they'd traveled on in Europe.

It was dark when the train pulled out of the station. Tomas sat close to the window so that he could watch the city lights.

"They're flickering!" he cried. They all noticed it. The flicker was intensive and made them screw up their eyes. "Why are they, Father?"

"The electricity must be on a different cycle than in Europe. I expect we shall get used to it."

"We shall have a lot of things to get used to," said Kristina.

When a man came into their carriage selling Coca-Cola and chocolate, they debated whether to break one of their dollars. They needed a treat, Kristina decided, and Coca-Cola was one of the things that Tomas had been looking forward to. They used to watch American soldiers drinking it.

Tomas was allowed to drink first. He tipped his head back and took a long swig. Then he gulped and almost retched.

6

"It tastes disgusting!"

"Let me try it." Astra took the bottle. She drank, and made a face. "It's hot, that's what's wrong."

"He must have had his crate beside the radiator," said Kristina.

They were unable to finish the bottle. What a waste of precious money! Tomas lamented the fact that they could have had chocolate instead. Or chewing gum. He went back to looking out of the window, straining to see what was out there. People were living in all those houses, Canadian people, speaking a language he could not understand. They would be speaking French, his father said, for this was French-speaking Canada, and when they came into Ontario, they would be in the English-speaking part. Toronto was in Ontario.

Tomas was watching a clothesline. He could see pillowcases, sheets, and shirts moving sideways. Now they were disappearing into the darkness one by one!

"Look, Astra—magic!"

She peered out. They were past now. But a few minutes later they saw another line of clothes, and they, too, were doing a disappearing trick.

"Must be somebody there," said Astra, "bringing in the wash, winding in the line or something."

"Perhaps some kind of pulley," suggested Hugo.

Tomas still thought it odd. The disembodied wash looked like ghosts dancing. He rubbed his eyes. They felt gritty. Everything had suddenly begun to seem strange and unreal. He was so tired; he hadn't slept much on the boat. He curled up in the corner and, in a moment, plummeted down into sleep, like a stone being dropped into a deep well. He dreamed that he was playing Ping-Pong with Zigi Jansons on a table that was rolling up and down, up and down. But, at the same time, he knew that Zigi was not there.

7

"Come on, Tom, up you go." He felt his father's arms helping him back onto the seat. He half opened his eyes. He seemed to have fallen on the floor. "Try to stop thrashing around, son!"

Astra, before drifting off to sleep, thought of her old friends and wondered what they'd be doing. Mara Jansons, her best friend from Latvian days, would still be at sea bound for Boston, Massachusetts. How miserable they'd been, parting from each other! It had been almost unbearable. They'd so much hoped to go together to a new country. They'd been friends since they could walk. Markus, her boyfriend at the DP camp in Esslingen, should be in Scotland by now, with his relatives. And other Latvians were going to Australia and New Zealand. They were being blown to all parts of the world, farther and farther from the country of their birth. Would they ever be able to return to it? And would she ever see her friends again?

Hugo did not sleep for a while. He wrote, in his head, a letter to Bettina Schneider, to whom he was betrothed and who lived with her mother and father in a small cottage near Hamburg. She had bright golden hair that curled around her head, making her look like a sunflower. He smiled as he remembered, and a catch came at the back of his throat. She was a bright, sunny girl, in keeping with her hair, with never a bad word to say about anyone.

The Schneiders had saved his life after he'd lost his own family. They had found him lying unconscious by the railway line and had taken him in. Bettina and her mother had nursed him through long, fevered weeks, not knowing who he was or where he had come from. They'd shielded him from the local Gestapo. He had lived with them for four years in all. They were his second family.

When they got to their destination in Toronto, he would put the letter to Bettina on paper and send it. He would do it immediately; he did not want her to think he had forgotten her. He never would, nor his promises to her.

His mind moved on to Toronto. They were being sponsored by a family named Fraser and would live on the top floor of their house. They had never met them. Ivar Fraser was half Latvian, on his mother's side. This must be the reason he'd agreed to sponsor them. Why else should he bother—for complete strangers? He was a teacher at the high school where their father would teach classics. Without an individual sponsor, they could not have come. There were government-sponsored projects, but their father would have had to go on ahead and take a job as a laborer at a hydropower plant or in a factory. Hugo doubted, though, that he would have been passed medically for manual work.

Their mother hoped to get a job too, teaching art. Then, with both parents earning—albeit less than Canadians—he, Astra, and Tomas would be able to go to school. After finishing, Astra hoped to go to a Canadian university to study languages. He himself wanted to train as a doctor and planned to return to Germany after a year to enter the University of Hamburg. He had promised Bettina that he would.

Astra yawned and sat up to exercise her neck and shoulders. The seats were not particularly comfortable. She caught Hugo's eye and winked. Then she settled down again.

It was so wonderful to have Hugo back in the family. She had to keep looking at him to make sure that he really was there and she was not hallucinating. During the four years that he'd been lost, she had felt as if part of her was missing. He would forget Bettina, given time.

He would stay with them—his own family—in Canada. He *could not* leave them again.

As they neared Toronto, they sat up straight and tidied themselves. They combed their hair. Kristina passed around a damp cloth for them to wipe their faces.

"We don't want the Frasers to think they're taking in a bunch of vagabonds!"

Astra had to tug hard to get the comb through her shoulder-length hair. Peering into a pocket mirror, she saw that it looked greasy and drab. Normally it was fair, as was Hugo's and Tomas's. It needed a good wash. Things like that had not been easy to do on shipboard.

She scrubbed with her finger at some stains on her skirt, but without success. She sighed. They must look just like what they were—DPs—displaced persons. She and Mara used to gaze with awe at the girls in the American magazines, with their gleaming hair and saucy, red-lipsticked mouths, and wonder if they could ever look like them. There were two buttons missing from her coat. They'd been missing when she got it from the Red Cross. All their shoes were scuffed and worn at the heels. The Frasers might take one look and decide not to claim them!

She glanced at her father and frowned. He was probably just tired, she thought uneasily. She saw that her mother was watching his face too.

"This must be Toronto," said Tomas, who had gotten up to stand at the window.

They were passing through suburbs. The young Petersons scrutinized the houses eagerly. Most were brick, a few wooden. They were set quite close together, even the bigger ones, and had unfenced gardens at the front. They all seemed to have basements. A number of houses had verandahs, some of which were white and curli-cued. Others had small porches.

"The Frasers must live in a big house, mustn't they," said Tomas, turning around, "if they're going to have room for us along with their own children. Don't you think so, Father?"

Lukas seemed not to have heard. He was looking around him as if he could not remember where he was or what he was doing here. He winced, as a spasm of pain contorted his face. He put a hand to his chest.

The train was slowing. They were pulling into a sta-tion. People were jumping up and dragging their bags from the overhead racks.

Astra and Hugo went to their father, and putting their hands under his armpits, raised him to his feet. He made no protest. He felt heavy and slack-limbed. They man-aged to ease him out of the compartment into the aisle. There was a steep step onto the platform. A box had been placed there to help passengers descend

"Careful now, Lukas," said Kristina, who was hov-ering behind.

He took a deep breath and stepped down onto the box; another, and he was on the platform. Out in the air, he appeared to steady himself, was able to stand upright. Astra and Hugo let go of his arms and went to pick up the luggage.

And then it happened. Their father suddenly doubled up and keeled over, right into the middle of the scurry-ing, disembarking passengers.

TWO

AFTER LUKAS'S COLLAPSE, everything happened very fast. Within minutes two men with a stretcher appeared, and a policeman, who moved the crowd back. Perhaps there had been an ambulance waiting. Perhaps this was not the first time that an immigrant had collapsed on arrival.

Lukas was lifted onto the stretcher, swaddled in blankets, and strapped down. The men then hoisted him up and set off along the platform, through the station, followed by Kristina walking very fast. Heads turned sympathetically to watch the little procession go by.

The twins and Tomas went to recover their luggage, which lay in heaps where it had been dropped.

"Quickly!" Astra was out of breath. "They might take him away, and we won't know where they've gone."

Tomas had not tied down the straps of his knapsack properly, and a box of paints, a sketchbook, and several pencils had spilled out.

"What an idiot! Pick them up, for goodness sake!"

"Don't shout!" Tomas glowered at his sister, who was less patient than her twin. "He's *my* father too!"

Astra crumpled and put her hands over her face for a moment. "I know. I didn't mean to shout, Tom. I'm sorry."

Meanwhile, Hugo was pursuing the rolling pencils and stuffing them, along with the book and paints, back into Tomas's bag. He glanced around. He frowned.

"Have you seen Mr. Fraser's camera?" They had bought a Leica for him as a present, had saved their money for months to do it.

"I was carrying it. I put it over there." Astra pointed across the platform. The place was empty now. "I'm *sure* I did. Somebody must have taken it! Do you think anyone could be as mean as that when Father was lying—?" She could not finish.

"Come on!" beseeched Tomas. "The camera doesn't matter any more."

"He is right, of course," Hugo said briskly. "Let's get a move on!"

He led the way. They ran, dodging around clusters of people, clutching their bundles. Tomas dropped one every few yards, scooped it up again, and then ran faster to catch up with his brother and sister.

The men were putting their father into the ambulance as they reached it. Their mother, her face as white as the clothes Tomas had seen in the dark, climbed in after them.

"Take care of yourselves, children," she said.

One man jumped out and secured the doors; then he went around to get into the driver's seat.

"Astra, ask where they're going!" cried Hugo, as the ambulance began to pull away from the curb.

She scrambled after it, waving her arms. "Wait! Please!" The driver saw her and rolled down his window. "Where are you going?" she asked, panting.

"Toronto General," he said, and wound the window

back up. Then he was moving into the mainstream of traffic, red light flashing and siren wailing. Astra burst into tears and turned her head away so that Tomas would not see her. But when she looked around, she saw that he was crying, too. She went to him, and Hugo came and put his arms around both their shoulders.

"This won't do," said Astra sniffling, lifting her head and drying her eyes. "We've got to be brave."

"I'm tired of being brave," said Tomas.

"I know—we all are." She rumpled his hair. "But not to be would be worse."

And then they remembered the Frasers. What *about* the Frasers? They might think they'd missed the train and gone home.

They had been sent a photograph of Ivar and Helen Fraser taken with their children, but that had gone in the ambulance in their mother's handbag. They went back into the station and walked about, eyeing everyone who seemed to be standing around waiting for someone or something. One couple in their mid-thirties looked likely.

Astra approached them. "Excuse me, are you Mr. and Mrs. Fraser?"

"*Who?*"

Astra wondered if she had said the name correctly. She had never heard it pronounced, had only seen it written. She attempted it a different way. "Fra—ser?"

"Sorry." The woman shook her head.

The station was busy, and there was a great deal of noise. Astra cocked her head, trying to catch the tail end of an announcement coming over the loudspeaker. She thought she had heard the name "Petersons." She stood still, listening as the announcement crackled overhead again.

"Would the Petersons family, newly arrived from

Quebec City and Cuxhaven in Germany, please go to the stationmaster's office."

"That's us! We have to go to the stationmaster's office. The Frasers must be waiting for us there."

A porter directed them.

Outside the door they paused to catch their breath, and Astra ran her fingers through her hair in an effort to tidy it. She straightened Tomas's jacket.

"It's okay," he grumbled, breaking free.

Hugo opened the door.

"Please let them be nice and kind," Astra prayed inside her head. "Please let them like us, and us like them."

Ivar and Helen Fraser turned out to be very nice people, and exceedingly kind. They welcomed the Petersons warmly and were most sympathetic and concerned when they heard about their father.

"How bad is he?" asked Ivar. He spoke some Latvian, though his wife did not.

"We don't know," said Astra. "We just don't know!"

As soon as they got home, Ivar promised, he would phone the hospital.

The Frasers lived on a tree-lined street in a quiet suburb, away from the throb of traffic. Their house was three stories, detached, made of red brick, with an open verandah on three sides. Two tall trees stood in the middle of the front lawn, and from the branches of one hung a thick rope knotted at the end. Tomas eyed it with interest. Helen said that their children had gone to visit their grandparents. Astra turned to her.

"Your house looks beautiful!"

"It's all right." Helen replied offhandedly and shrugged, while eyeing her husband.

Astra saw the look exchanged between them but could

not comprehend it. Was there anything wrong? Astra dismissed the thought. She was on edge—how could she not be, when her father might be dying?—and as a result she was beginning to imagine undercurrents when probably none existed. She must stay calm, so that she could cope better with whatever had to be coped with. They had learned that early on in their life as refugees.

They went inside. The hardwood floors were all polished; bright rugs lay scattered about. But the walls were completely bare, which was strange. Astra noticed that there were rectangular marks outlining places where pictures or mirrors must have hung. Perhaps they were getting ready to redecorate.

"Come into the kitchen and get warm," said Helen, "while Ivar phones the hospital. I'll have some food ready for you in a moment."

The kitchen was cheerful, yet managed to be serene at the same time. Set on the pine dresser were dishes in a blue, white, and yellow pattern. A vase of bronze chrysanthemums gleamed on the window sill. Astra had the impression that a happy family must live in this house—except that the wall shelves were bare, and there were boxes standing in a corner. She had that same feeling of disquiet, though she tried not to let Helen see her staring at the boxes.

"Would you like some soup? Tomato? Do you fancy that?" Helen was asking gaily. "And how about some ham sandwiches?" They could see that she wanted to cheer them up, and they struggled to respond.

"That would be nice, thank you," said Astra politely. She was not at all hungry, but she thought it might be rude to refuse food. She could not take her eyes off the door.

When Ivar Fraser came in, she leaped up.

"How is he? Is he—?"

"He's still alive," said Ivar gently, "but very seriously ill. It was a heart attack—you realized that."

"Can we see him?" asked Hugo.

"I doubt if they'll let you in. But I'll run you over to the hospital later, so that you can see your mother. I've sent a message to her to say that you are with us."

"You are very kind, Mr. Fraser," said Astra.

"Not at all." Again, he and his wife exchanged that look. It puzzled Astra greatly, and troubled her. "And please do call us Helen and Ivar," he added.

"Ivar," said Hugo hesitantly, "the hospital bill? For father?"

"It's all right—don't worry! It's all taken care of!"

Was Ivar paying? He must be. How much would that be? The questions were too difficult to dwell on now.

After they'd eaten, Helen took them upstairs. The rooms on the top floor had dormer windows. There were three, apart from the little kitchenette and bathroom: a bedroom for their parents, one for the boys, and a living room that would also be Astra's bedroom. There was a studio couch for her to sleep on. Helen apologized for that.

"I don't mind in the least. It will be marvelous. We've had to sleep in all sorts of places!"

"I'm sure you have. You've come through so much. And here we have been living a life of comfort!"

"That's not your fault. It's just luck, isn't it?"

Helen nodded. "I guess so." She had a most engaging smile. She was undoubtedly a good woman. Genuinely good. It stood to reason that both of the Frasers must be.

Ivar had written them that his mother, who had died last year, had been most distressed by Latvia's fate. Her brother and his family had been taken away to Siberia by the Soviets and had not been heard from since.

"Ivar was very moved by the letter your father wrote

17

to the school asking for help," said Helen. "The principal showed it to him, knowing he was half Latvian. We were only too pleased to be able to do something for you."

She told them where the bathroom was on the lower floor, said there was plenty of hot water, and left them to unpack.

Astra showered, washed her hair, and put on the string of amber beads she'd brought with her from Latvia. They'd belonged to her great-grandmother. The feel of the beads against her throat comforted her a little.

"This is a fantastic house," declared Tomas. "I'm going to like it here." Then he remembered, and his face clouded over. "If Father gets better, that is. He *will* get better, won't he? Won't he, Hugo?"

"I expect so," Hugo lied. His heart felt like a great big stone lump in his chest. He knew from the way Ivar Fraser had spoken that there did not seem to be much hope for their father.

They went to the hospital in the afternoon. Their mother looked drained. Astra and Hugo sat with her in a small room and talked in low voices. Tomas had come in for a few minutes, then Ivar had taken him off to the museum. From beyond the door came the swishing sound of rubber-soled feet passing in the corridor, and the quiet clink of instruments in other rooms. Hospital noises. It was very warm and airless.

"He's holding on," their mother told them. "But he's very low, and unconscious most of the time. And when he does open his eyes, he doesn't seem to know me. Poor Lukas!" Her voice broke.

"Cry, Mother, if you want to," said Astra.

She and Hugo sat with their arms around her, holding

her shaking body against theirs. They had taken on the role of the parents now; they must be the ones to try to offer comfort and reassurance after so many years when it had been the other way around. They said that their father was strong, a fighter who did not give up easily.

"He didn't give up when he was wounded by the Cheka and lost a great deal of blood and was very weak, did he?" said Astra. "He was at death's door for weeks, remember! But he rallied, didn't he?"

"He was younger, that makes a difference. And in the years since then his constitution has weakened, what with all the physical hardships and the constant worry."

"You worried too," Hugo reminded her.

"We must not give up hope," said Astra.

"I do not intend to, dear."

"I'm sorry, Mother, I didn't mean to sound—"

"That's all right." Kristina touched her hand. She was calm again, and in control of herself. She took down her hair and reknotted it at the back of her neck. Strands of silver had begun to appear among the fair ones.

Astra and Hugo tried to persuade her to come back to the Frasers' with them for a little while, but she would not leave the hospital and Lukas.

"You'll call us if anything changes?" asked Hugo.

"Of course. And now I am going to go and sit at his bedside and think positive thoughts about him. Perhaps I can transmit them to him!"

"We will think good thoughts too," promised Astra.

"I am glad at least," said Kristina, "that the Frasers are such good people. To know that we have a home with them is one worry less."

The house was filled with the smell of cooking. Helen set a huge roast beef on the table. The Petersons had not seen such a large piece of meat for a long time, Tomas exclaimed aloud. Helen smiled and served him first, giving him a huge helping. After today, thought Astra, we must start to cook our own meals upstairs; we cannot expect the Frasers to feed as well as house us.

But they had only the money given to them on arrival, apart from some deutsche marks that they had saved to bring over. She did not know how long they would last. She did not know how much anything would cost. They had expected their father to start work at the high school and earn money right away. That, of course, was out of the question now.

"Eat up, Astra!" Helen smiled at her. "Aren't you hungry?"

"Oh yes, yes I am."

Astra struggled to finish the food on her plate. They all did, Tomas too. They were not used to such large meals. But they had been taught to leave not even a scrap on their plates, to waste nothing. Who knew where the next meal might come from? Tomas thought of abandoning a slice of meat and a potato, but seeing Astra's warning eye on him, he gave up the idea. She could be a pain at times and was getting far too bossy for her own good!

After the main course came apple pie and ice cream. Astra requested just a little but still received a large slice of pie, served with what seemed to her to be a monstrous scoop of ice cream.

"Take your time," advised Ivar.

"I think I shall burst," announced Tomas, when he finally laid down his spoon. Ivar smiled and translated what Tomas had said into English for Helen's benefit.

"It was delicious, thank you, Helen," said Astra, and

she got up to gather the plates. She felt bloated, had eaten far too much.

"Leave those!" said Helen, nodding at the dishes. "You've had enough for one day. Oh, and by the way, you're most welcome to use my washing machine. It's in the basement."

They'd seen many photographs of these machines in magazines.

"We'll need to buy one of our own, won't we, Astra?" said Tomas.

With what? she almost retaliated, checking herself in time. It would be too leading a question, too awkward for everybody. Her head ached, as well as her stomach. She went upstairs, lay on the couch, and stared at the sloping ceiling.

Tomas followed her up.

"Want to play cards, Astra?"

"Not just now, Tom."

He rummaged and found the pack of cards, which were creased and well used from countless journeys. He laid them out on a small table for a game of Patience. Zigi's mother, Olga, had taught him to play Patience. He sighed. He wished Zigi were here now.

Hugo, left downstairs, went out on the verandah to see if there were any stars. Would the night sky be different here from what it had been over Europe? It seemed not. That was a relief. He needed something to be constant. It was a crisp, clear night, good for seeing stars. There were the seven stars winking away in Orion's belt. He and Bettina had often gazed at the sky together. Tonight, though, he could not think of her. The one thought that filled his mind and pounded in it like a giant pulse was that, less than four weeks after being reunited with his father, he might lose him again. This time, forever.

"It's not fair!" he wanted to shout up to the stars. It was what they used to say when they were young and something had gone wrong.

He stayed outside until he began to feel chilled, then he came back into the warm kitchen and closed the door. He went into the hall. The Frasers must be in their living room at the front of the house; he could hear the murmur of their voices. He saw that the door was very slightly ajar.

As he started up the stairs, he heard words that made him stop dead.

"We'll have to tell them sooner or later."

His understanding of English was not good, but he was fairly sure that that was what they had said.

Tell them *what*? Hugo tightened his grip of the bannister. He should move on; he should not stay to eavesdrop. Eavesdroppers never heard good of themselves, it was said. He strained to listen.

"Not yet though, Ivar. How can we? I mean . . . under the circumstances . . ."

"I know! What terrible bad luck . . ."

"What a mess! And we can't really afford . . ."

Hugo went on up the stairs. He would not tell Astra what he had overheard. There was no point in adding to their worries. He was going to try to forget the Frasers' conversation. Anyway, perhaps he had been mistaken. It was terrible not to know a language properly and to be constantly worrying whether you had picked up the correct meaning. To miss even one word could lead to all sorts of misunderstandings.

Tomas looked up as he came into the room. "Want a game, Hugo?"

"Okay!"

"Astra?"

22

"Oh, all right. Might as well. It'll help to pass the time."

They sat around the low table. Tomas shuffled the cards over and over again, until Astra said she thought that would do. He began to deal.

"You *do* like the house, don't you, Astra?" He paused to look at her. "You want to stay?"

"Of course I want to stay. Where else would we go? Anyway, I think it's great. Who wouldn't?" She spread her cards into a fan and frowned. "How come you always deal me dud hands, Small Brother?" She rearranged a card. "No, I like the house, and the Frasers are lovely; they couldn't be more generous, but—"

"But what?"

"Oh, I don't know." She shrugged. "I just have the feeling that things are not quite what they seem."

THREE

"THERE IS SOMETHING we must tell you," said Ivar, a few days later. During those days, the Petersons had trekked up and down to the hospital, learning to take the dark red and yellow streetcar and go by themselves while Ivar was at school, fearing each time they reached their destination that bad news might be awaiting them. They seldom spoke on the journey, sat staring out into the unfamiliar city streets.

They were beginning to find their way around. As Hugo said, it was not difficult. The streets were straight and intersected one another at right angles, forming a grid. Some, like Yonge Street and Bloor Street, stretched for miles from one end of the city to the other, and beyond. There were no nooks and crannies. These streets were quite unlike the narrow winding ones of old Esslingen that Astra and Tomas had been used to walking. Astra missed the sight of old buildings and the sense that people had trod the same paths for hundreds of years. She found these thoroughfares too open and thought a lot of the buildings looked shoddy.

Tomas eyed the few high buildings with interest. He'd been hoping to find a real jungle of skyscrapers jabbing up to the sky and was a bit disappointed. He would have to go to New York for that, Ivar said, though he was sure that, in the years to come, they would see many more high-rise buildings shooting up in Toronto itself.

Lukas Petersons had swung up and down as he fought for his life. One night the children had been called urgently to the hospital, and they'd gone, thinking the end had come, but he had rallied. And now he seemed to have stabilized, even improved a little, although he still needed round-the-clock nursing. They were allowing themselves to hope a little.

Astra and Hugo were sitting at the kitchen table, drinking coffee with Helen and Ivar. Tomas had gone down to the basement with the Frasers' nine-year-old son Gary to play with his train set.

"Yes, I'm afraid we have some not very good news for you," said Helen.

It is coming, Hugo thought calmly, whatever it is.

The Frasers talked slowly and distinctly so that Hugo could follow.

"It is hard to have to tell you this," Ivar began, "but, you see, we are not going to be staying in Toronto. We are moving to Alberta. Very soon, in fact."

"Ivar has a new job in Calgary. That's out west. It's a promotion for him, he will be vice-principal at a school."

There was silence while Astra and Hugo digested this news and its implications for them. The Frasers would be moving; they would no longer be living here, in this house. Astra's and Hugo's eyes strayed to the boxes in the corner. They made sense now. And the blank spaces on the walls and the empty shelves. The Frasers were moving to Alberta, wherever that was. But the Petersons could not expect to move with them. The twins looked at each other.

Where would *they* go?

"Ivar couldn't really afford not to take the job," Helen went on.

"Of course not," said Hugo. "I know a job is an important thing."

"It came up ages after we'd agreed to sponsor you."

"We understand," said Astra.

"Ivar has to start after Christmas—the previous vice-principal died suddenly. But we're going to have to move before then. The people who've bought our house made us a very good offer, but they've insisted on having possession the first week in December."

"Next week!" Astra exclaimed.

"But don't worry!" said Ivar. "We have found somewhere else for you to live."

"It's not—well, maybe it's not quite as nice as our house." Helen was apologetic. "But I'm afraid it's all we've been able to find. It's near the university and not far from the hospital. You'll be able to walk from there."

"It is kind of you to bother so much about us." Astra could hear her own voice emerging polite and stilted. The news had struck a chill into her, made her feel as if she'd been turned into a block of stone. The easy intimacy that had developed between her and Helen seemed to have evaporated. But it was not the Frasers' fault. It was just a combination of circumstances, as always. And here were the Frasers, who owed them nothing, feeling embarrassed and guilty because they could not keep them in their house! What a burden they were! Part of her was grateful for the generosity shown to them by everyone, another part raged against having to be at the receiving end of charity all the time. As soon as possible, she vowed to herself, they would stand on their own feet. She saw the same resolve in Hugo's face. They had always been able to read each other's minds. They were in tune. Between them, they could hold the family together.

"The rooms we've found for you are in the house of my brother Mike's mother-in-law," said Helen. "They're in the basement. Accommodation is not easy to come by in Toronto these days—the city is growing so rapidly. And they can't build new houses fast enough."

Astra said quickly that she was sure the rooms would be fine as long as there was somewhere for them to sleep.

Hugo was frowning. "The rent? Money for rent?"

"I shall pay." Ivar's embarrassment increased. "I'm your sponsor, after all!"

"That doesn't mean you should pay for everything," said Astra.

"No, but in this case—well, I don't think you are in a position to pay it yourselves, not right now. And since I'm your sponsor, I'm responsible for you for the first year." Ivar was trying to speak lightly. "I can't leave you out in the street or let you starve!"

Hugo thought of his father being tended twenty-four hours a day in the hospital by a team of highly trained nurses. "The hospital bills must be big."

"Now I've told you before—don't worry! It's all part of the deal. It's what I agreed to take on."

We can't really afford . . . Hugo remembered the words he'd overheard. When the Frasers had offered to sponsor them, they had not expected to have such a big problem on their hands. They had not expected to have to support a sick man. After all, they had had medical checkups and X rays before they left Europe and had been declared fit. Hugo wished there was something he and Astra could do. But what? They couldn't pay the hospital bills, nor could they take their father out of the hospital and let him die.

The Frasers were not so very well off, apparently, not in North American terms, although it seemed to the Petersons, coming from a DP camp, that they lived like millionaires. Astra had understood this through talking to Helen. A teacher's salary in Canada was not considered very large when it came to supporting a wife and family. They had been able to afford this house only because Ivar's parents had left him some money when they died.

"We'll take you over to see your new place tomorrow evening," said Ivar, "and to Meet Mrs. Craik."

When they went upstairs, the twins sat down on the couch to discuss this new development. Hugo took off his glasses and rubbed his eyes. It was a habit that he had when he was worried. They agreed that they had no other choice at the moment but to allow Ivar to pay their rent and their father's hospital bills.

"We'll pay him back, though," vowed Hugo "no matter how long it takes."

Astra nodded. "And we must find work. Doing any-thing—anything at all."

It would mean abandoning their education, at least for the present—though perhaps not forever. Everyone said that in North America you always had the chance to move on, as long as you were prepared to work hard.

It was evening when Astra and Hugo saw their new rooms for the first time, so it was difficult to tell how

28

much natural light they would get. Not much, they guessed. There were only two rooms, one very small with two couches, and the other a little larger with two more couches, a fold-up table, four upright chairs, and one armchair covered in wrinkled, yellowish beige cloth. All the colors were drab: sludge browns, olive greens, and sad fawns. The general effect under the electric lights was depressing, and their spirits sank.

Everything was relative, Astra told herself. They were feeling this way because they had come from the Frasers' house, which was light and colorful. If they had come straight from the boat, with its cramped spaces and narrow bunks, they would have felt differently. Once they got used to them, these rooms would be all right. They would have to be.

What did worry her was that there was sleeping space only for four. Was it presumed that their father would not be coming home? Or was it just that the Frasers had been unable to find three rooms for them anywhere else? As they'd said, accommodation was difficult in the city, with new immigrants arriving every week.

"The two boys can sleep in the little room," said Mrs. Craik. She was a small, plump woman and walked on high-heeled shoes, with her toes turned out a bit like a pigeon. All three Petersons had disliked her on sight, not because she was small or plump or because of the way she walked. They disliked her because of her smile. It was a turned-on smile made by her mouth but not her eyes. They'd all noticed it right away.

"Pleased to meet you," she said, not pleased at all.

Her eyes were small and sharp—and watchful, darting here and there, missing nothing. She could not really have wanted to take them in. Ivar must be paying her well. The thought was an uncomfortable one.

"And the sitting room will be for your parents." Mrs

Craik tugged the olive green curtain across the window but not enough to hide the brick wall of the house next door. "That is of course *if* your father—well, I mean . . ." She coughed and continued, turning to Astra, "My daughter Shirley has very kindly offered to take *you*, dear."

"To take *me*?"

"Yes, isn't that good of her? They have a lovely large house in a real snazzy neighborhood. It's called Forest Hill. That says it all, doesn't it? What a lucky girl you are, Astra! Mike is doing pretty good at his work, isn't he, Helen? He's in the car business. Shirley is willing to give you bed and board in return for a little help."

Helen intervened. "With the children, Astra. To baby-sit, that's all."

Astra nodded. She did not know what to say. She did not want to live apart from her family. Their mother had started to come home at night, now that their father was no longer in immediate danger.

"You can stay here until your father is allowed home, Astra," said Ivar. "Then, after that, well, perhaps you wouldn't mind going to live with Shirley and Mike? There isn't *quite* enough room here for five."

Mrs. Craik's lip curled, though not into a smile. She said rather pettishly, "Oh, I don't know if that'll suit Shirl. She was expecting Astra to come next week, otherwise she'd have gotten herself another girl."

"We'll sort it out." Helen jumped in again hurriedly. "I'll speak to Shirley."

With a slightly martyred air, Mrs. Craik showed them the rest of the apartment, as she called it. "The kitchen!" she announced, opening the door of a cupboard in which there was a hot plate, an electric kettle with a frayed cord, and three pans on a shelf.

"We know it's not very big—" Helen began, but was interrupted by Mrs. Craik.

"I don't suppose they are used to *big* kitchens," she said icily, and closed the door.

There was also a bathroom, with a sink, and a separate shower screened by a plastic curtain that had gone moldy around the bottom. They would have to wash their dishes in the bathroom sink, fetch water for cooking from there too. Well, that was not so terrible. At least there was water. And a regular toilet. Their rooms occupied half the basement; the rest was taken up by Mrs. Craik's own laundry room. She did not invite them to use it.

It was decided that the Petersons should move in next weekend so that the Frasers would have a few clear days in which to pack up their house.

"I don't suppose you'll have much stuff?" Mrs. Craik smiled her smile.

"No, not much," Astra said.

"Don't let Mrs. Craik get you down!" said Helen. "She's not as bad she seems." She did not sound convincing.

Astra was not worried about Mrs. Craik getting her down. During the past four years they had had to deal with camp commandants, Gestapo officers, women in white coats delousing them with harsh brushes, Russian and German soldiers waging war. Mrs. Craik would not come anywhere near measuring up to any of them. But it would have been pleasanter—and easier—if she could have been as nice as Helen.

"Now if you have any problems, you must write and tell us," said Ivar. "I shall still be your sponsor, and there to help you." He had an unsealed envelope in his hand, which he passed to Hugo. "I want you to take this. And please don't protest! It's the least I can do to help compensate for pulling out on you like this."

From the envelope Hugo drew five one-hundred dollar bills.

"But we cannot—!"

"I said don't protest! It's for emergencies, and it's a gift—not a loan. Take it as a gift from my mother, from the money she left me. I know she would want you to have it. And I'll give you the addresses of a couple of old Latvian friends of hers. They're elderly but you may like to look them up."

In the face of such generosity, the Petersons were speechless. But they were in no position to reject it. Haltingly, they tried to convey their thanks. Ivar waved them aside, smiling.

Helen gave them clothing. Ivar was bigger than the two boys, so his clothes hung loosely on Hugo and almost drowned Tomas. Astra said she could make some alterations. In Latvia she had never liked sewing, but years of being a refugee had forced her to learn how to use a needle and thread.

Her problem with Helen's clothes was the other way around, for Helen was small and slightly built. But she accepted the sweaters, even though they were too tight under the arms, and the skirts, even though they were too short. She might come across another immigrant girl who would be grateful to have them, or she might even be able to make an exchange.

The Petersons packed their bags yet again, thanked the Frasers yet again, and said good-bye to Helen and the children. They promised to write, keep in touch, never to forget them, and then were driven by Ivar to their new dwelling place. Not *home*, thought Astra; she could not think of it as that.

In the daytime the basement looked even drearier. The light filtering in from outside was thin and grayish.

Ivar hugged each of them before leaving and said again how sorry he was things had turned out this way and that he had not been able to arrange something better for them.

"You must not be sorry," said Hugo. "You have enabled us to come to Canada. You have given us a chance."

After Ivar had gone, they went out for a walk. They could leave by a basement door, so did not have to go through Mrs. Craik's part of the house.

The street, even to their eyes, appeared run-down. Garbage cans stood in front of some of the houses. Paint on doors and windows was flaking. The curtains at the windows looked soiled. Weeds grew high in the gardens and around the front steps. It did not seem a likely place for Mrs. Craik.

Helen had told them that the street had gone down in recent years. When Mrs. Craik had first moved in as a bride, it had been in better shape. Now a lot of the houses were being used as rooming houses.

"She's watching us," whispered Tomas.

Glancing around, Hugo and Astra saw the woman's face at the window of one of the lower rooms. She was holding the net curtain aside. She made no attempt to hide the fact that she was watching them.

"There are people like that in every country," said Astra.

"She's a witch," Tomas declared in a loud voice to the street in general.

Astra hushed him.

"She doesn't understand Latvian, does she?"

"That's true!"

They laughed.

"There are *some* advantages in being Latvian!" said Hugo.

"I'll be able to call her what I like, and she won't know." Tomas's eyes gleamed.

"You must be polite to her now, Tom," his sister warned him. "She might not understand Latvian, but she'll be able to tell if you're being cheeky by the tone of your voice. And if she doesn't like us she could put us out."

"There's no chance of her *liking* us. Well, is there?"

The next day was a happier one. When they arrived at the hospital, their mother told them that they were to be allowed to see their father.

"Just for ten minutes or so. We mustn't tire him."

He was lying propped up against a pile of pillows. They were shocked to see how wasted and bloodless he looked. And his beard seemed to have gone totally white. He held out thin hands to them. They went to take them, and sat on the edge of the bed holding onto him, unable to say anything for the first few minutes.

"You gave us a shock, silly Papa!" Astra then said softly.

"I gave myself one." His voice was weak. Kristina watched anxiously, though she sat very still on the upright chair. She was not a woman to fuss about. They noticed her sketchbook on the window sill. She took it with her wherever she went and had made a visual record of all their wanderings. She must have spent many hours in this room, drawing their father's face as it had gone through its numerous changes.

"Now tell me about our new home," he requested.

Tomas was getting ready to open his mouth. Astra

forestalled him, saying, "It's very central. We've got two rooms, our own shower, and our own entrance."

"Good, good."

"It's near the university," said Hugo.

"Excellent. That will be handy for you and Astra next year."

"We may have moved by then, of course," Astra put in quickly.

"We'll see. We may have bought our own house, eh? Who knows! Once I get my strength back and get started at the school . . . But I look forward to coming home and being with you all again."

After fifteen minutes a nurse appeared in the doorway and indicated that it was time to go. They kissed Lukas and followed their mother out.

She had an appointment to see the doctor and said they should come with her. Tomas too. Although he was only twelve, he had never been kept out of family consultations.

The doctor was a Scotsman called Dr. Andrew. He shook hands with them all vigorously.

"You've had it rough, haven't you. What a start for you in a new country! Now I'm going to speak bluntly to you about your father. Stop me if you don't understand! My accent might be difficult for you." And he laughed.

They sat on the edge of their chairs, leaning forward slightly, listening carefully.

"Your father could go home in a week or so, but he'd have to be careful. *Very* careful. It would be better if he could stay longer in the hospital or go into a convalescent home. Convalescent," he repeated. "You understand?" They did not know the word in English, and he had to explain.

"Ah, a rest home." Kristina nodded. "Lukas could do with that. Our rooms are not very warm."

"But that would cost more money, wouldn't it?" asked Astra.

"Oh, indeed. Now I know your bills are being paid by Mr. Fraser—"

"But we don't want him to have to pay more than is necessary."

"I'm sure not. Your father will still need medication, but if he could go home, at least there'd be no more hospital bills."

"We have to take him home."

"Do you feel you could look after him yourselves?"

"We will look after him," said Kristina. "We will manage to keep him warm."

"That's fine, then. Anything else you'd like to ask?"

"Yes, please." Hugo paused in order to find the English words. "Our father has a job, in a school, to teach Latin and Greek. He is very keen for this job. When do you think—?"

"He'd be able to work?" Dr. Andrew sighed. "I'm afraid there's not much chance of him ever being able to do that, lad."

"*Never?*"

"You'll have to face the fact that he's going to be a semi-invalid. It was a massive heart attack, and he's lucky to be alive. It was sheer determination that pulled him through, if you ask me. But he's not going to be fit enough to do a full-time job ever again."

FOUR

T HE FAMILY brought Lukas home two days later. They took him in a cab. The distance was short, so the fare was small. They had to keep track of every cent. They had been walking everywhere. Ten cents saved on the streetcar was ten cents worth saving. They had resolved not to break into the Frasers' five hundred dollars unless it was absolutely necessary, which it soon might be.

Mrs. Craik came to the front door when she saw the taxi stopping in the street. She watched while Astra and Hugo helped their father out. She did not miss his uneven gait, the way his feet stumbled on the path. He straightened his back to greet her. He needs a walking stick to lean on, thought Hugo. He is a proud man who hates leaning on anyone, even us.

"I'm honored to meet you, madam." Lukas bowed to Mrs. Craik, who was unused to European ways and looked at him suspiciously. "It is most kind of you to take us into your home."

Mrs. Craik nodded. Was she softening a little? Most people did, faced with Lukas's courteous manners.

"Most kind," repeated Lukas.

Mrs. Craik found her tongue. "I'm a Christian woman and would never see anyone left out on the street."

Hypocrite! thought Astra. Mrs. Craik had warned a vagrant off their patch of street only the day before. He'd been fishing through the garbage cans, reminding Astra of how they'd done that themselves in Germany. She'd felt for him. A bum, Mrs. Craik had called him. A good-for-nothing low-down bum. Astra hated their landlady. The dislike had been instant and mutual. Mrs. Craik appeared to think that, because they were DPs, they should grovel.

Tomorrow, Astra was due to move to her daughter Shirley's house. Mrs. Craik had told them that five was too many in the basement, and she couldn't allow her house to become overcrowded. To become a slum! There was no point in arguing. Mrs. Craik had the upper hand, and she knew it. Astra suspected she enjoyed having them in her power. Perhaps Tom had been right when he'd called her a witch!

Lukas was exhausted by the time they got him into the basement. He agreed to go to bed at once, without protesting. It was then that they realized how difficult it was going to be. He was too tired to have them around talking and making noise. He needed peace and quiet.

They had had the electric heater on since early morning to boost the tepid air that was coming through the heating grille in the wall, but even so, he was shivering. Kristina spread another blanket on top of him, and Astra filled a second hot water bottle. The central heating in this house did not seem to be as efficient as it had at the Frasers', or else Mrs. Craik did not keep the furnace stoked so high. How warm and comfortable they'd been at the Frasers'! It had been like a taste of paradise. So far the weather had been reasonably mild, but everyone said that after Christmas it could be fiercely cold and drop to as much as twenty or thirty below freezing. They had been surprised to hear the weather in Toronto could be so cold. When they'd looked it up on a map, they had seen that it was almost on the same latitude as Rome. But the winter temperatures would certainly not be the same.

The three young Petersons went out. They had spent long hours roaming the streets looking in shop windows, or wandering through the big department stores like Simpson's and Eaton's. Their eyes were dazzled by all the gleaming new things that they might buy—when they had money. "Look at that!" they kept saying. "Look—over there!" Astra had begun to notice the assistants in the stores eyeing them. They must appear odd, with their handed-down, ill-fitting clothes. And they only looked, never bought. They never touched anything either, were careful not to. They were terrified that they might be suspected of stealing. They had no rights in this country; they were not citizens.

Earlier Tomas had picked out a shiny red racing bicycle that cost fifty-four dollars and fifty cents. Hugo coveted a pair of binoculars, among other things, and Astra's eyes were dazzled by the array of clothes for sale. And nothing was rationed! The only thing they needed was money.

"People must be rich here," said Tomas.

"Not everyone," said Hugo. "The people on our street are not. By the way," he added, "I've found a job. I start in January." He had gone off by himself for a couple of hours the previous afternoon, without saying anything. He kept things more to himself than did either Astra or Tomas, who in that way were more alike; they had to tell everything.

"A job!" repeated Astra, a little annoyed that Hugo had not told her. Once, he would have kept nothing from her. "Doing what?"

"Construction. On a building site. Ninety cents an hour."

"Construction! Oh, Hugo, it will be hard work. And outside, too. In the freezing cold." She did not mention his headaches. He had always been prone to them, and his head wound had not helped.

"What else can I do? My English isn't good enough for office work. And I have no qualifications."

Astra wondered what she could do to earn money. If she worked hard, might Shirley pay her a wage, as well as give her food and lodging?

They were passing a grocery store when Tomas, who was walking on the inside, close to the windows, stopped abruptly. "Wait a minute, you two!" He pointed at a notice taped to the window and read aloud in English, "Boy wanted." There was a word before "boy." "What does that say, Astra?"

"Delivery. They want someone to deliver groceries."

"Me!"

He dashed inside, followed more slowly by the twins. The store was small, dark, and cluttered; it smelled of coffee, cheese, and salami. Big glass jars of pickles glinted on the shelves. Ribbons of sausages hung suspended from the ceiling, some so low that the Petersons had to duck their heads. The grocer was a small man, with frizzy gray hair; a long white apron wrapped around his waist reached almost to the floor. He turned out to be Polish, and his name was Mr. Zawacki.

Astra helped Tomas negotiate with him. His English was not a great deal better than Tomas's.

"You want a job?"

"Yes."

"How old?"

"Fourteen."

"Huh!"

40

"Almost."

"Saturdays, and after school. You go to school?"

"In January."

"You ride a bike?"

"Oh yes! I get a *bike*?"

"Bike with carrier. Groceries go in carrier. Come!"

Mr. Zawacki took them through the back to the yard. The bicycle was the usual type, of course, not a racing model, and a bit rusty around the spokes. The heavy, slack chain looked as if it might be prone to slipping off. But, still, it was a bike. Fixed to the front was a large metal container.

"How much will you pay?" asked Astra.

"Twenty-five cents an hour."

"That's not much."

The grocer spread out his hands. "Plenty boys will do it."

"*I* will do it," said Tomas, trying to count in his head how many hours he would have to work to save fifty-five dollars. He figured it to be two hundred and twenty!

"Twenty hours a week," said Mr. Zawacki.

Tomas did another sum. In eleven weeks (if he didn't spend anything on other things) he could have the bike. He could have it by spring.

"Start tomorrow. Okay?"

"Okay!" said Tomas.

Helen's brother Mike came to pick up Astra in the morning. He was driving a brand-new Pontiac. Tomas whistled and went out into the street to examine it. He loved cars. Mike opened up the hood and let him look inside.

"I never know what car Mike will arrive in next!" Mrs. Craik gave a tinkly laugh. "He's got so many."

Astra did not feel like laughing. I'm being silly, she thought. I'm going only two or three miles away; I'll

41

still be in the same city. But she was so used to living close to her family, often all of them in one room, that it felt like an enormous wrench.

"It needn't be for long, Astra," her mother said quietly. "When we get some money together, we will move out of here and find a place of our own. Hugo will be earning soon, and once your father is a little stronger, I shall look for a job too."

Astra kissed her father on the forehead.

"Be good, Papa! No running around the block now!"

He caught hold of her hand and squeezed it. There was not much strength in his grip. He made her think of a faint, flickering flame that could be extinguished in a sudden rush of wind.

"I'll see you tomorrow." She planned to come home each day. She could easily walk the three miles.

Hugo went up to the street with her.

"Now if you don't like it, you're to come back!"

"And sleep where? With you and Tomas? Old Craik would have a fit."

Mike's and Tomas's heads were invisible behind the hood of the Pontiac's engine. Mike was explaining what the parts were, repeating the English words. Distributor. Battery. Spark plugs. Tomas was trying to say them after him. Mike seemed easygoing, a pleasant, hearty sort of man. Astra felt somewhat reassured.

She felt less so when she met his wife, Shirley. She was a younger version of her mother, in appearance and mannerisms, and the moment Astra saw her standing at the door of her expensive "snazzy" house, holding a squalling baby in her arms, she felt her spirits take a downward swoop.

"Where have you been?" Shirley snapped at Mike. "You've been gone for ages. You know I've got a hair appointment at eleven." Then she remembered Astra and smiled as her mother did, using her mouth only. "So you're Astra! Hi! Come on in and meet the family."

Apart from the red-faced infant, who was called Gregory (after the film star Gregory Peck), there were a two-year-old with the name of Deanna (after Deanna Durbin) and a three-and-a-half-year-old named Clark (after Clark Gable). They were fighting for possession of a toy Indian, who had been scalped in a previous battle, no doubt. Clark won, and Deanna began to scream.

"Cut that out!" commanded their mother.

The children paid no attention.

"I'll be off to work then," said Mike, and disappeared out the door.

"Typical! Honestly, men! I'd have nothing to do with them if I was you. Cars and baseball—that's all he cares about!"

Shirley skirted around the two older children, who were still tussling, and led Astra up the stairs to her bedroom. It was small but warm and attractively furnished with flowery prints, and it had a view into the backyard, which was ringed with tall fir trees. The room cheered Astra. It would be nice to have a space of her own, somewhere she could retreat to and read in peace, write letters, relax.

"Want to hold the baby a minute?"

Shirley dumped Gregory into Astra's arms. He felt hot and sweaty, and he smelled, strongly.

"I'll just show you the kids' rooms and where everything is in the kitchen. You know how to make up a formula?"

"A formula?"

"Milk for the baby's bottle. You just mix powder and water."

Astra shook her head.

"It's easy, don't worry! You'll soon get the hang of it. Just make sure before you feed Greggie that you try the milk on the back of your hand. You don't want to scald him, do you?"

Astra looked down into Greggie's outraged face. She did not know what she wanted to do with him. Not hold him, that was for sure. She had never been particularly fond of small children, not like Mara, who doted on them and had virtually brought up her small sister Klara. What a pity Mara was not here! Not just to hold the baby, but to talk to. Astra longed for a good long heart-to-heart talk with her old friend.

Shirley set out the tin of formula on the kitchen table, and a can of Campbell's tomato soup.

"There's bread in the bin." She glanced at her watch. "Glory! I'll need to fly. You be okay now? See you later! See you, kids. Be nice to Astra."

A flurry of high heels, a banging of the front door, and she was gone, leaving behind only the whiff of her rather sweet perfume. Deanna and Clark quieted down, the baby did not.

"Greggie needs his diaper changed," remarked Clark. "He's stinky."

He and Deanna made a great fuss of showing Astra where to find clean diapers and the zinc ointment. They squatted close to her and watched while she inexpertly performed the task. At one point the baby rolled off her knee to land with a soft bump on the floor, whereupon he redoubled his screaming.

"He don't like being dropped," said Clark. "He might get deaded." His eyes glistened. He had his mother's and grandmother's cold ice blue eyes. Astra knew that *they* would not be friends. The other two children looked more like their father, plump-faced and rosy-cheeked. Deanna nestled into her side and stuck her thumb in her mouth.

Astra mixed the milk formula and heated the soup. After being fed, Gregory and Deanna both fell asleep, leaving Astra to play quoits and ball with Clark.

Shirley returned in the late afternoon. She hadn't meant to be so long, she said. She'd been delayed—she did not say with what.

Astra had her meal in the kitchen with the children: wieners and Heinz beans. She was hungry, could have eaten more, but did not like to ask. Shirley did not eat; she sat beside the table, with her legs crossed, smoking a cigarette, exhorting Deanna every now and then not to cram so much into her mouth. She explained that she and Mike liked to eat later, when the kids had gone to bed. Mike needed to relax after a hard day. They usually took trays into the den.

"Den?" Astra repeated.

Shirley laughed. "Oh, nothing to do with animals! Gee, it must be hard for you not being quite able to latch on to things. I guess you've got a lot to learn. A den's a little living room," she explained in a voice that she might use to one of her children. "It's a snug kinda place. We like to relax in there in the evening. Mike's thinking of getting us a TV—we'd be the first on the block to have it!"

Astra helped Shirley bathe the children and settle them down in bed.

"It might be a good idea to leave your door ajar at night," said Shirley, "so you can hear the baby. See you in the morning!" She tripped off down the stairs.

Astra sat on the edge of her bed. She appeared to have been hired as a nursemaid, even though she was untrained and completely inexperienced. She was sure that

45

Helen had not realized that. But she was certainly not going to write and tell her. She would just have to make the best of it.

She was too tired to read. She fell asleep on top of her bed, fully clothed, and wakened sometime in the middle of the night to the sound of Gregory roaring. She had no watch, so could not tell what time it was. Confused, disoriented, she stumbled out of her room and bumped into Shirley on the landing.

"Didn't you hear him?"

"Sorry."

"I'll get him, now that I'm up!" Shirley sounded as if she was in a vile temper.

She was still in it in the morning—Astra was to learn that this was her usual start-the-day mood. She stood by the stove cooking sausages, bacon, and eggs, banging the frying pan about, and cracking the eggs sharply against its side. The smell made Astra's mouth water. She had brought the children, whom she had managed to dress without too many disruptions, down into the kitchen. Mike was sitting at the table, in his shirtsleeves, reading last night's *Toronto Daily Star*. She had been reading back copies of it herself, and the morning paper, the *Globe and Mail*, to help improve her English and to find out what was happening in the city and the world. She always scanned the papers for news of the Baltic states, but they were never mentioned. It was as if they had vanished from the face of the earth, which they had, in a way. They'd been swallowed up by the Russian giant.

"Hi there, Astra!" Mike lifted his head. "How're you doing? Get a good sleep?"

"Yes, thank you."

"You don't have to ask if *he* did," Shirley said to Astra. "He sleeps through anything. They could drop a bomb in the backyard, and he wouldn't wake up."

She scooped the contents of the frying pan onto a plate—two slices of bacon, two sausages, and two eggs—and slapped it down on the table in front of him. Then she dished gray, lumpy oatmeal into three bowls and put them in front of Deanna, Clark, and Astra. She poured herself coffee and lit a cigarette.

"I can't stand food in the morning," she told Astra. "I don't know how he can bear to eat bacon and eggs, do you?"

Tomas was enjoying his grocery rounds. Mr. Zawacki would give him some broken biscuits or a candy bar for his pocket.

"So that you ride fast!"

Sometimes, too, the customers would give him something to eat or a drink of homemade lemonade. Old ladies living alone were particularly good that way. They wanted to talk to him, and to hear about his experiences as a refugee. Many had been refugees from Europe after World War I and still talked with marked accents. Others—Jews mostly—had fled Hitler's Germany in the thirties, before World War II started. The immigrants didn't like Canadian food: soggy white bread, orange cheddar cheese, and hamburgers! They liked rye bread, pickled herrings, pickled cucumbers, and cheeses with subtler tastes. In the district Mr. Zawacki served, there seemed to be more immigrants than native Canadians. But even those so-called natives had been immigrants, too, at one time, as Mr. Zawacki pointed out to Tomas; they had come from Britain—England, Ireland, Scotland, and Wales.

"They all speak English. So we must speak English, whether we like it or not!"

Business was good; Christmas was coming. The customers were buying extra groceries, boxes of cookies, and cans of fruit in syrup, putting them away for the big celebration. They were baking cakes with currants, thick brown sugar, sticky cherries, and shelled nuts. Tomas's carrier was heavily laden.

At the end of the week he received his first five dollars. He'd been thinking about the money all afternoon.

"Watch you don't lose it!" said Mr. Zawacki.

Tomas folded the bills carefully and put them in his back pocket.

He took the route home that led past the bicycle store. There it was—the one that he would buy! He stood close to the window admiring it, fingering the money in his pocket. His breath smeared the glass, blurring the bike.

"You're late!" His mother was dishing out the meal when he came in. Potatoes, cabbage, and one wiener each. Sausages again! Tomas almost said, but stopped himself. Wieners were cheap.

His father and Hugo were already seated at the small table. It seemed odd not to see Astra there. She had come home twice, with three dreadful small children in tow— Mrs. Craik's grandchildren, though Mrs. Craik hadn't seemed all that pleased to see them. She'd sent them back down to the basement after ten minutes, which had meant that Astra couldn't stay long, as the noise was too much for their father. Astra had told Hugo that she hated it at Shirley's house, but they were not to tell their mother.

"Come on then, Tom, sit down!" His mother looked tired. She usually did these days, was often awake during the night, with their father.

Tomas pulled up his chair. There was barely room for them all at the table; their elbows banged, and their knees bumped.

"So, Tom, how was work today?" Lukas inquired. He

was gaining in strength each day, just a little, but enough to hearten them.

Tomas slid his hand into his back pocket and brought out the five dollars.

"Ah, so you've been paid! You are rich!"

Tomas's hand tightened over the five crisp bills for a moment; then his fingers slackened, and he let the money drop onto the table. He pushed it across to his mother.

"What's this?"

"It's for you. For the family. To buy food and things."

"But your bike, Tom?"

"I'll get it some day. I *want* you to take it, Mother."

"Well . . ."

"Please, Mother!"

"Very well." She gathered up the bills and put them in her apron pocket. She smiled. "Thank you, Tom. They will be useful. It is good to have sons working for the family."

Astra was allowed to come home for Christmas Eve. *Allowed*. Shirley did not use the word when she said Astra could go, but that was what she implied. She was not pleased, however, as she and Mike had an invitation to a party, and now she would have no baby-sitter.

"How am I to get a girl on Christmas Eve, tell me!"

"I don't know." Astra stared back at her stubbornly, unprepared to give way on this issue. Her family always celebrated Christmas Eve together. They had a special meal, lit candles, sang carols, exchanged presents, and, at midnight, went to church. Shirley said Canadians had their dinner and gave out their presents on Christmas Day.

"We are Latvians."

"You'll need to change your ways if you want to fit in here."

"I don't see why. What we do in our own home is our concern."

"That's the trouble with you DPs—you think your ways are better!"

When Shirley was in a bad mood, she lashed out at whoever was closest. Astra was learning to ignore it, though it was not always possible to stay calm when she was being insulted. Shirley would ridicule her for not knowing what some things were on the shopping list. "Ajax!" she shrieked, when Astra came back without it. "Everybody knows what Ajax is!" I know he's a hero in Greek mythology, Astra wanted to say, but she knew it would only inflame Shirley further. Shirley was a stupid woman. Reminding herself of that helped Astra to stay calm. Shirley went on, "Everybody knows Ajax is a cleanser! Haven't you got any eyes in your head? Can't you read?" Sometimes Astra would go up to her room and punch her pillow hard.

At other times Shirley could be friendly and would chat with her as if she were a close friend. She would show off her new clothes when she brought them home and ask Astra's opinion. And she gave her a couple of dresses (which were not really Astra's style, being flouncy and low-cut at the front or back) and a pair of red, lined boots. The boots were too tight, but Astra wore them, glad of their warmth.

On Christmas Eve, in spite of her pique, Shirley handed a parcel to Astra.

"For your family. For Christmas."

"Thank you. That is very kind."

"I just love giving things to people. Mom says I'm far too extravagant."

Astra had not received any wages. It seemed that she was expected to look after the children seven days a week in return for her room and food. Perhaps this was how things were in Canada. If so, it was not for her to challenge it.

When she took Shirley's parcel home and unpacked it, she found it contained four cans of bright green processed peas and two of Campbell's soup.

"It's not a very Christmasy sort of present, is it?" said Tomas.

"We shall use them, no doubt." Kristina put the cans in the cupboard. "But not for Christmas."

Tomas had received gifts from his customers: chocolate and cookies, tangerines and nuts, and tips of twenty-five and fifty cents. And the Frasers had sent a huge box of crystallized fruits and a bottle of sherry.

"We hope you have a very merry Christmas," Helen had written on the card.

For dinner they were having roast pork with sauerkraut. In Latvia they had always had a pig's head also. Pigs were considered lucky. And Kristina had made the traditional pepper cookies spiced with ginger, as well as pepper, and cut into different shapes like hearts, stars, and circles.

Hugo and Tomas had been busy decorating the room with fir branches, and Mr. Zawacki had presented them with six tall white candles. The candlelight made the room seem softer, and the sweet smell of the fir reminded them of their Baltic home. And on the window sill, flanked by two candles, stood the small Latvian flag that they had brought with them on their journeys—two horizontal stripes of dark red with a narrower white band in the middle.

Lukas raised his sherry glass.

"Draugiem dzimtenē!" To absent friends!

Lukas and Kristina fell silent. Astra wondered whom

they were thinking of. Probably their grandmother, left behind in Latvia.

Tomas thought of Zigi Jansons, from whom he'd had a card of a robin standing on a snowy branch. Zigi had written inside: "America is great! See you."

Astra thought of Mara, from whom she'd had a long letter. The Jansons seemed to be doing well; Paulis' job as school janitor had worked out; Olga was also employed at the school, as a cleaner; Mara was working in a laundry; and they liked their apartment. They had met some other Latvians. Everyone was kind.

Hugo thought of Bettina and her parents. He thought of them in their little cottage, with the stove burning brightly and the tree in the corner ablaze with candles. He had received an air letter from Bettina. She said that she had sent by sea mail a blue woolen sweater that she had knitted herself. It would take some weeks to come. He could imagine her sitting by the stove, her hair gleaming, the needles flashing, as her hands worked deftly. In her letter she had also told him that she missed him. "We all miss you, Hugo. But we hope you are well and happy. We send Christmas greetings to your family." Although Hugo was happy to be with his own family, he felt a strong pang of homesickness for the Schneiders' cottage, and for Bettina.

"*Draugiem dzimtenē*," the five Petersons repeated, each thinking his or her separate thoughts.

They drank.

"And now, to us!" Lukas raised his glass once more. "Let us be grateful that we are all together again."

FIVE

IT WAS RAINING on the day that Hugo started work, and freezing. As soon as the rain hit the ground, it froze. He put on an old pair of Ivar Fraser's corduroy trousers rolled up at the bottom, his heaviest sweater, and the only jacket he had, a fur-trimmed, fake leather one that Frau Schneider had bought for him in Hamburg.

"And your gloves," his mother reminded him. "Don't forget your gloves! And your hat!"

He put on the leather hat with the flaps that came down over his ears. He had bought it at the Salvation Army store for fifty cents.

If he had forgotten either gloves or hat, he would have remembered them as soon as he put his nose out of the door. The morning was dark, as well as cold. A horse-drawn milk cart was clopping along the street. Nothing else was moving. The horse's breath puffed white into the air. The driver sat crouched over the reins, head down.

Hugo set off to negotiate the icy sidewalks. He slipped, slid, and lost his footing on a corner. He went down on to his back with a sharp crack. For a moment he lay winded, then he scrambled up, reflecting that it would not do to arrive injured on his first day at work. He felt his back. Little harm seemed to have been done. He continued even more carefully.

Arriving at the site, he went to report to the manager. He was busy with someone else, and waved Hugo away to a shed.

"You'll find the other guys in there."

Opening the door of the shed, Hugo stepped back as thick fumes of cigarette and cheap cigar smoke hit him in the face. Through the haze he saw a number of men sitting hunched over hot mugs of coffee. Some of them lifted their heads to eye him, others did not bother. One man grunted, but whether it was meant to be a greeting or a noise of complaint Hugo could not be sure.

He continued to hesitate on the step.

"Come in if you're coming in!"

"And shut that damn door!"

Hugo did as he was told and pulled the door shut behind him. There was little room for him and, immediately, he wished that he had stayed outside. He was being looked over.

"DP?"

Hugo nodded.

"Where you from?"

"Latvia."

"What?"

Hugo repeated the name of his country. His country! He could scarcely imagine it anymore. The name did not seem to ring a bell with the men. He was not surprised. The Petersons had found that many Canadians had only a rough idea of the map of Europe and were particularly vague about the Baltic.

"Which side were you on during the war?"

"No side."

"Come on! Everyone was on a side. I fought in Europe, nearly got it in the Ardennes from a Gerry shell—so I should know!"

Hugo was sweating. The stuffy heat of the shed and the cross-examination from this burly man with bullish shoulders and huge hands were bringing on a headache. He took off his glasses and rubbed his eyes. How could he begin to explain the complicated history of the Baltic states—battered by everybody, torn apart by bigger powers? How could he explain in his halting English? He felt as if he had a knot in his tongue.

"Lay off the kid, Hank," an older man in a plaid jacket said. He turned to Hugo. "What's your name?"

"Hugo."

"Hugo!" Hank snorted. "Sounds like a Gerry name to me. Hope you're not a Nazi!"

"Don't be stupid!" The older man intervened again. "They wouldn't let Nazis into the country."

"Don't you be so sure! They're letting in all sorts of riffraff. Don't know what they think they're up to. Before we know it, you and me'll be out of a job. Though could be that I won't have to worry much about little Hugo." He pronounced Hugo's name in a way that made fun of it. "Hugg-o!" He snickered. One or two of the others joined him. "Ever handled a pickaxe, Hugg-o?"

Hugo thought he was going to disgrace himself by fainting, when the door opened at his back and a gust of cold air blasted through the shed.

"Okay, guys!" The site manager stood there stamping his feet and flapping his arms. "On your way."

Grumbling, they filed out. Hugo remained beside the shed, waiting to be told what to do.

The manager jerked his head, indicating that Hugo should follow him. He'd told him, when he'd gone for the job, that the work consisted of renovating an existing restaurant, and building three shops with apartments above on an adjacent site. He'd told him the work would be outside, and was not for weaklings.

He led Hugo over to the restaurant and explained in a few short words what he was to do, put a chisel into his hands, then left him.

Hugo surveyed the wall. He was to take the old mortar out from between the bricks with the chisel; that was all. It must be the most boring job on the site, but at least he should be able to do it. He had had to lie to get the job, to say that he had had experience in the construction industry.

He raised the chisel and struck at the mortar. The blunt-edged blade skidded down the wall dislodging little of the gray filling. His hands felt numb. He struck again. Not much happened. At this rate he'd never earn his ninety cents an hour. The rain had not let up. He felt the icy drops oozing down between the flap of his hat and his collar.

"Here, let me have that, Hugo!"

He lifted his head to see the man with the plaid jacket. He had a shovel over his shoulder.

"Give me the chisel!"

The man put the shovel against the wall and took the chisel out of Hugo's hands. "Move in closer to the wall, boy, come in at a sharper angle. You'll get the hang of it in no time."

Hugo thanked him and tried again, with a bit more success.

"Just keep at it. And don't let the other guys bother you. One or two are a bit on the rough side—I'd steer clear of them if I was you. My name's Bob, by the way. If you want to know anything, just ask me." He picked up his shovel and went on his way.

Hugo attacked the wall with renewed vigor. Thank goodness for Bob! He'd been thinking he would be lucky to last the day when Bob had come by.

At noon they broke for lunch for one hour. It had taken Hugo half an hour to walk to the site, so there was no question of his going home. When he straightened up, he saw that his jacket and trousers were covered with blobs of ice. He brushed them off with his hands as best he could. His shoulders felt locked, and his wrists ached.

And he was ravenous. His stomach was growling like a mad dog. He had brought with him two slices of white bread with processed cheese in the middle. He gulped down the sandwich so quickly that he hardly tasted it. Tomorrow he'd bring more. He had not reckoned on the enormous appetite working manually, and out-of-doors, would give him. The other workers had huge lunch pails with them and flasks of soup and coffee.

They were eating their lunch in the shed. Hugo did not go in. He went, instead, for a walk, and in the next street came upon a library. The sight of it brightened him. He pushed open the door. The warmth and quiet that engulfed him, and the smell of the books, made him smile. Then he looked down at his clothes and saw that he was covered with mortar dust. He must look like a tramp! He tried to dust himself off, but the dampness was making the dirt cling. He noticed that the girl behind the counter was eyeing his clothes too.

"May I help you?"

"Well, no—I don't know."

"Do you want to join the library?"

"Yes, yes please."

She gave him a form and helped him to fill it in.

"Hugo Petersons," she read.

"I'm from Latvia," he said quickly. "One of the Baltic—"

"I know where it is! My mother is Estonian."

"She is?"

She nodded, smiling. Her name was Irena. She had been taken to Estonia for a holiday when she was a small child, though remembered little about it other than that there had been fine white sand at the seaside and tall fir trees around her grandmother's house.

"And now we can't go any more to see her! And you can't go to Latvia, can you?"

They talked so long that Hugo was almost late getting back to the site. He decided he would go each day to the library at lunchtime, sit in the warmth, and read. It would be something to look forward to. And the girl—Irena—did not seem to mind that his clothes were dirty.

When five o'clock came, he found he could barely move. His back ached. His arms ached. His shoulders ached. You'd have thought he was an old man! It took a few minutes before he could stand fully upright. He rotated his shoulders, moved his head gingerly from side to side, flexed his right arm. He would be as stiff as a ramrod in the morning.

The site manager had come around to inspect his work. He stood there pursing his lips.

"Bit slow, aren't you?"

"I will get quicker."

The man nodded. "I don't mind taking on DPs. Usually find you're hard workers. See you tomorrow."

"I shall be here."

"Good night, Hugo!" Bob gave a friendly wave as he went by.

58

"Good night, Bob!"

Turning, Hugo saw Hank and one of the other men approaching. When they were almost level with him, Hank took the cigarette stub from between his lips and put it into his mouth, ashes and all. Hugo blinked. Hank chewed for a second or two, then spat. The contents of his mouth landed on Hugo's boot. The men laughed and moved on.

Another worker was hanging around the gate. Hugo eyed him warily. The man seemed to be waiting for him. He had a lean face under his fur hat, and dark eyes. As Hugo passed, he fell into step.

"They say you are Latvian?" He spoke with an accent. Hugo saw that his eyes looked intelligent, and friendly. "I am from Lithuania." He introduced himself as Kostas Adomonis. He had not been in the shed in the morning; he said that he had little to do with his fellow workers. Some of them were all right; others were best avoided. He had been in Canada for more than a year, had come over as a government contract worker. He'd been given a job in a meat packing company out in Alberta, in the skinning department.

"As soon as the year was up, I quit."

"You didn't like the job?"

"We had to work with electric knives—they were heavy, like twelve, thirteen pounds! We had to skin calves. I had never done anything like that before. In Lithuania I was a lawyer. It was terrible work—you had to hold the knife in one hand and pull the hide off with the other. By nighttime my arm would be swollen up like a balloon."

When Hugo got in, he found his parents waiting anxiously. They wanted to hear how he had fared on the construction site. Was the work hard? How had the other men treated him?

"Everything was okay."

"You don't look okay. You can hardly move." Kristina had to pull off his boots, his hands and arms were so stiff. She fussed, massaging his feet. "The work is too much for you."

"No, it's not!" Hugo said cheerfully. Better to have to scrape out old mortar from between bricks than skin calves.

Tomas couldn't eat any breakfast on the day that he started school.

"You'll be hungry in the middle of the morning," his mother warned him. She made up some sandwiches for his lunch and put in a banana. It was Tomas's favorite fruit. They hadn't seen a banana from the beginning of the war until they'd arrived in Canada. Now they could buy a pound for only nineteen cents!

"What is the English word for *'vēsture'*?" Tomas asked his father. He felt suddenly panicked. The little English that he knew seemed to have gone from him.

"History. Say it, Tom. His-tor-y."

Tomas said it slowly and carefully.

"I am the new student," said Lukas, and again Tomas repeated the words. "Miss Lawson is my teacher."

"Miss Lawson is my teacher."

"There's no time now for English lessons!" Kristina put Tomas's lunch into his bag. "You don't want to be late the first morning. Would you like me to come with you?"

"Of course not!"

"Remember that you have to report first to the principal's office."

"Good luck!" his father called after him.

A few flakes of snow were drifting down over the

street. Tomas fastened the flaps of his hat under his chin. He didn't want to get frostbitten ears. Winters had been cold in Latvia, but this kind of cold seemed to bite deeper into you. If he ran, he would warm up faster, but he didn't feel like running. He'd get to school too quickly.

He didn't know why he should feel so bothered about starting a new school. He'd gone to plenty of different ones, and sometimes to none at all for weeks on end. That was what was worrying him, he supposed; that he had missed so much schooling during the war. After it was over he had gone to the Latvian school in Esslingen. He was bound to be hopelessly behind. He kicked a stone in his path, sending it shooting up the sidewalk. When Hugo had taken him along to the school to be enrolled, the principal had said they were putting him in with younger children because of the "language problem." What if they were really young—babies!

The fact that all the classes would be in English was another thing that was bothering him. The idea of thinking in English all day long tired his head. "I am the new student," he repeated to himself. "Miss Lawson is my teacher. I like to do math-e-mat-ics and his-tor-y."

Always before, too, he'd had Zigi to go with. They hadn't cared about being new boys. They would stick together at recess and look out for each other. He missed Zigi terribly. He missed the good times they'd had together, roaming the countryside from first light to dark. So much had happened to the two of them together. They'd narrowly escaped death when they'd been fishing on the riverbank and American planes had come over to bomb the German defenses. They'd run for their lives, with bullets bouncing around them like huge hailstones!

So busy was he with what was going on inside his

head that he arrived at the school before realizing it. The yard was full of kids yelling and chasing one another. Like at any other school anywhere—except that they were yelling in English.

He hung around outside the gate until the bell rang and the kids rushed to line up at the two doors. One was marked BOYS and the other GIRLS. In Esslingen they had all gone in at the same door.

A man appeared at the boys' door, a woman at the girls', and a hush descended. The children began to march inside, swinging their arms like soldiers. *Tramp, tramp, tramp* went the feet. The lines dwindled. When only the very last stragglers were left, Tomas slipped inside the gate and crossed the yard.

He had memorized the way to the principal's room. He was good at finding his way around places. Buildings interested him. He even thought he might like to be an architect when he grew up.

He knocked on the principal's door. Nothing happened. Had someone called out on the other side of the door? But if so, what had they said? He knocked again. The door opened.

"I said 'Enter!' " The principal, whose name was Mr. Phillips, stopped when he saw Tomas. "Ah, it's our new boys, isn't it? From Latvia?"

"Yes. My name is Tomas Petersons."

"Welcome to our school, Tom." Mr. Phillips smiled at him. Tomas relaxed a little. At least Mr. Phillips seemed to be a nice man. "You're going to be in Miss Lawson's class. You know that, don't you? That's grade six. The children will be about a year younger than you, but that's not much, is it?"

"Yes."

"You think a year is a lot?"

Tomas was confused. He felt heat surging into his face. "No, I think no."

"Never mind!" Mr. Phillips patted him on the shoulder. "It'll all seem easier in six months' time. Come on, I'll take you along to your room. Room 7."

As they approached Room 7, they heard a great din coming from it. It seemed that the class was shrieking with laughter. Mr. Phillips frowned and hurried ahead of Tomas into the room. Suddenly the noise subsided. Only one pupil remained out of his seat. A boy with a shock of black hair stood behind the teacher's desk, with a wastepaper basket raised above his head. He stood there frozen, like a statue. He must have had the basket over his head, and perhaps had been capering about—that would explain the merriment.

With a great scraping of chairs, the rest of the class stood up and chanted in singsong unison, "Good morning, Mr. Phillips."

"Good morning," he barked. He turned to the boy with the wastepaper basket. "Put that down, Taylor!" Taylor put it down. "Come here!" Taylor came. "How *many* times have I had to warn you?" Taylor said nothing. "Come with me!" said the principal, and he marched off into a side cloakroom, pulling a long, coiling leather strap from his pocket as he went. Tomas's eyes widened. Mr.Phillips seemed to have turned into a different kind of man—a red-faced man with blazing eyes. Taylor followed him with his head down. There was not a sound in the classroom.

They listened as they heard the swish of the strap, then the crack as it met its target, and Taylor's cry. The strap whistled four times.

"Please, sir, *please* sir!"

"Get back to your desk!"

Taylor came running into the room. He went straight down the aisle to his desk, and put his arms on its top, cradled his face in them. His shoulders shook. Some of the other boys were smirking, Tomas saw. He felt shocked. In Latvian schools children were not beaten. He was going to hate it here. Hugo was lucky to be old enough to go and work on a construction site.

"Where is Miss Lawson?" Mr. Phillips demanded.

"She had to take Alice Jones out 'cos she said she was going to throw up," one girl volunteered.

"I don't want one single movement out of you until she comes back. Do you understand? And if any of you don't understand, you'll get the same as Taylor."

"Yes, sir," they chorused.

"Get your primers out and read silently." Mr. Phillips turned to Tomas. "Miss Lawson will be back soon." Then he left the room.

Tomas remained where he was, in full view of the class. Rows of eyes were fastened on him over the rims of books. He stared away, examined the blackboard. "Spelling" it said at the top, followed by a list of words. "Admire, admirable, admiration . . ." The only noise was that of Taylor's sobbing.

There was a little ripple of sound as Miss Lawson entered the room, followed by Alice Jones, who, apparently recovered, went bouncing to her desk with a look of importance. Tomas was to learn that Alice Jones liked attention. Miss Lawson, he was glad to see, was young and pretty. Her face was pink, and Tomas wondered if she had met the principal in the corridor and been bawled out by him.

Miss Lawson looked at him. "Hello there."

"I am the new teacher," he said, and the class broke into spasms of laughter. Tomas wanted to drop through the floor.

64

"Quiet!" She frowned at the class. Then she smiled at Tomas. "*I* am the teacher. I think *you* must be our new pupil, Tomas Petersons."

She gave him a desk near the front, next to a boy with sandy hair and a freckled face. His name was Sandy, too. Sandy Campbell.

"Sandy will look after you," she said.

At recess Tomas followed Sandy out into the sheds.

"I'm from Glasgow—that's in Scotland. I've been here for a year."

"You like Canada?"

"Aye, it's great!"

"Are you refugees?"

"Refugees? Naw! My dad came over because he could get a better job. He's an engineer. What does your dad do?"

"Nothing at the moment. He's sick."

A group of boys had gathered around. One asked, "Do you speak Latin?"

"*Latin?* No—Latvian."

"What's it like in Latvia?"

Tomas shrugged. "There are trees. Birch trees. Fir trees."

"Is that all? Do you sleep in beds?"

"Of course we sleep in beds." Tomas was indignant.

"Don't be so ignorant," Sandy told the boy who had asked.

"Who are you calling ignorant?" The boy, who was bigger, pushed Sandy in the chest.

Tomas immediately went to his new friend's aid, and it was thus that he returned home from his first day at school with a pulsating black eye.

Astra was tired. She had been up half the night with the baby. He was teething. She had rubbed soothing gel on

65

his gums, which had not done much to soothe, rocked him in her arms, walked him up and down. He'd finally fallen asleep around five, and at six-thirty Deanna had jumped on her stomach, demanding she get up.

All three children were in fretful moods that day, reflecting her own state. It snowed off and on, and Clark had a cold, so they couldn't go out. Shirley disappeared midmorning to get her hair done and to meet a friend for lunch. Before she left she told Astra to give the kids an early meal. She had visitors coming for dinner and wanted the kitchen clear for cooking. She was making steaks, with lemon meringue pie for dessert.

In the late afternoon, heaped together on the couch, Astra and the three children fell asleep, and wakened only when Shirley opened the door and put the light on.

Befuddled, Astra shook her head, waiting for the storm to break over it.

"Haven't you fed those kids yet? I *told* you to feed them early, didn't I? *Didn't* I?" Shirley's voice rose to a screech.

Astra stood up and smoothed down her skirt. "Yes, you did," she said calmly.

"And why didn't you do it?"

"I fell asleep. I was exhausted. I had hardly any sleep last night because of the baby."

"Do you realize that it was ten to *six*, and I have guests coming at seven?"

Deanna began to cry.

"It's straight to bed for all of you! You can have corn flakes in your room, and that's all!" Shirley turned her furious look back onto Astra. "And you can get the kids to bed double-quick and come help me in the kitchen!" She swung around on her heel and stomped out of the room.

Astra went after her.

Shirley was unpacking a bag of groceries on the kitchen table. Her fury had not abated. "Didn't you hear what I said? Are you deaf as well as dumb?"

"I heard very well. And you can go feed your own kids and put them to bed. You think that I am a slave, but I am not!"

"What an ungrateful little brat!" For a moment Astra thought Shirley was going to take a swing at her. Her arm started to go up, and then she seemed to think better of it. Astra was taller, leaner, and certainly stronger. "When I think what I've done for you—taken you in, given you a good home, given you clothes, fed you—!" Shirley spluttered until she found her tongue again. "Who do you think you are, anyway? You're nothing! *Nobody*."

She paused to let her words sink in. From the living room came the cacophony of sound made by three tired children crying. Astra pushed the door shut with her toe. She looked Shirley straight in the eye.

"You've exploited me, and you know it."

"You're fired! Do you hear—*fired!* You can go in the morning."

"I wouldn't stay another ten minutes in your house— not even if you paid me! And I know there's no chance of that."

Six

ASTRA REALIZED from the moment that Shirley screamed "You're fired!" that more trouble would lie in store. There would be Shirley's mother to contend with, too. News of her dismissal preceded her, and by the time she arrived home, having lugged her bags down to the main road in a temperature of ten below and on and off a bus and then a streetcar, her family knew all about it. Or at least Shirley's version.

"You poor girl!" Kristina helped her off with her coat. "Come and sit in front of the fire. You look frozen stiff."

Astra felt frozen. Her coat was a summer one, given to her by the Red Cross in Germany; it had a V-neck, which left her throat and chest exposed to the bitter cold. Kristina put a blanket around her shoulders, and Hugo brought her a cup of hot chocolate.

"I thought Mike would have driven you home," said Lukas. "*He* seemed to be a decent man."

Mike had offered when he came in, but Shirley had shrieked at him, "Don't you dare—not after what she's done!" He had looked embarrassed, had tried to mutter some sort of apology. He had been cut off by his wife, who had seemed on the verge of hysterics.

"She sounds unbalanced." Kristina was rubbing Astra's hands, trying to warm them. "I'm glad you're out of her house."

"But where are we going to live now?" asked Tomas, before his mother could stop him.

"Live?"

Lukas sighed. "We had better tell you, Astra—Mrs. Craik has given us notice to go. But it is not your fault, and you are not to feel that it is."

"Mrs. Craik was fizzing, like fireworks." Tomas grinned at the recollection. He was sitting at the table struggling with English grammar homework. "I kept thinking her head would blow off." He had not been able to understand every word Mrs. Craik had said, but it had not mattered. He had discovered that he could understand a lot of what people said just by watching their faces.

"But we don't have to go until the end of the month," said Kristina. "So we have two weeks in which to find something else."

Tomas thought that they should write and tell Mr. Fraser about Mrs. Craik. "It would serve her right! She shouldn't get away with it, should she? After all, he's paying her rent money for us." Lukas said that he would write, but only *after* they had found somewhere else to go.

"We must not bother the Frasers if we can avoid it." They had weekly letters from either Helen or Ivar asking how they were faring.

"But she might write to them first and blame us." Tomas felt furious at the thought of it.

"We'll have to risk that. Anyway, I doubt that the Frasers would take her word over ours."

Tomas frowned at his homework notebook. What was a demonstrative adjective? He wasn't sure that he could even say the word "demonstrative" properly, and Astra was in no state to be asked. He'd probably get nothing out of ten for this day's homework and be put back to the grade below. By the time he came home from his delivery rounds and had his dinner, he felt too tired to concentrate. Sandy had said he shouldn't let Miss Lawson know that he was working after school. Mr. Phillips might not like it, might try to stop him. Sandy wasn't sure if you were allowed to have a job when you were only twelve years old. Sandy's father thought that Tomas shouldn't be working, but then, he was an engineer, with a job, and didn't understand.

Something else was bothering Tomas. Tomorrow was St. Valentine's Day and it seemed that the boys were expected to send cards to the girls. To say they *loved* them!

"You're joking!" he'd said to Sandy. "Cards with *hearts* on them?"

Sandy had looked uncomfortable. "It's not serious. It's more a joke." He was sending one to a girl named Carol. Tomas thought he was crazy. Sending a card to *Carol!* She and her friend Helen sat in front of Sandy and Tomas. She was forever turning around in her seat and swinging her long, fair pigtails to and fro. They had colored bows on the end, a different color each day. She did it deliberately, to be annoying, Tomas thought. He was tempted to tie the braids together and anchor them to the back of her seat. The swish-swish of those tails of hair irritated him.

"I am not sending a card to any silly girl!" he'd declared. "I don't care what the rest of you do." He did care what the rest of them did; that was the trouble. He didn't like standing out

"Tom, have you finished that homework?" his mother asked. "It's time you went to bed."

He yawned and had another go at the demonstrative adjectives. "Make up a sentence using a demonstrative adjective." He chewed his pen, then wrote, "This boy is tired." You could say that again!

Hugo took the cup out of Astra's hand. She was amazingly silent, for Astra. He put the back of his hand against her head. It felt on fire. Kristina went to wring out a cloth with cold water, to lay on her brow.

"Astra can sleep in my bed," said Hugo. "I'll be okay on the floor. And tomorrow I'll start looking for another place for us."

"But you're at work all day, Hugo." Kristina did not add, "And you come home exhausted and fit for nothing!" But he knew that that was what she was thinking.

The next morning Astra herself was fit for nothing. She had a raging temperature, and her chest ached unbearably, especially over the breastbone. Perhaps she'd gotten frostbite there, she tried to say with a smile, but did not quite manage it. She almost fainted when she stood up. Hugo helped her into the living room, where Kristina tucked her into the couch she had just vacated.

"You can lie there beside your father! Two beds in a row! This is getting to be like a hospital ward."

"I could go for a doctor," Tomas offered.

His mother gave him a look that told him not to pursue the topic. Doctors cost money. In the DP camp there had always been doctors around, and if you were sick, they treated you for nothing. There it hadn't been so important to have money. Here it was very important.

They needed money to rent rooms. Tomas munched his corn flakes and pondered. The world seemed upside down. Leipzig, near where they had lived in a barn for

71

the last few months of the war, was now in East Germany, on the other side of the Iron Curtain. It wasn't a real curtain—everyone called it that because it was as if a curtain made of iron had come down to cut Europe in two. Soldiers with guns and steel bayonets patrolled the borders to keep their people in. Latvia was one of the cutoff countries. Their father badly wanted to go back and see his mother, who was old and ailing. He fretted about her. But there was no going back through the curtain. If you did, they'd grab you and keep you.

"Tom, you'll be late for school!" His mother cut through his thoughts.

He put on the parka that Hugo had gotten for him in the Salvation Army store for two dollars. He was pleased with the parka, which was in good condition and came down almost to his knees. It was blue and had a quilted lining, a zipper up the front, a zippered front pocket, and a fur-trimmed hood that you could take off if you wanted to. He didn't want to take it off on a day like this. It was cold outside, and he hurried along as fast as he could, slipping and sliding on the icy patches.

The school yard was full of squawking, giggling kids, huddled in groups. There were a lot of white envelopes about, some being flaunted, others half concealed. Tomas then remembered about the stupid Valentine business.

"Did you bring one?" asked Sandy.

Tomas shook his head. "You don't *have* to, do you? It's not like homework?"

" 'Course not." Sandy had one sticking out of his parka pocket. Yet he was always saying that girls were pains in the neck!

Tomas changed the subject and told Sandy that he had to find somewhere for his family to live.

"*You* have to?"

"Astra—she is sick—and Mother must stay with her and Father. And Hugo is working all day."

Sandy pulled two licorice sticks from his pocket. He usually had some kind of candy. He gave one piece to Tomas, who, for a moment, allowed himself to forget his family's problems and enjoy the sweet, slightly bitter taste of the licorice. Sandy was a good pal!

The bell began to ring, and they went to join their line.

"So I do not know what to do," said Tomas. "To find a place. I do not know how to look."

Sandy nodded. He and his parents and younger sister lived in a nice house—a whole house—with a basement, two other floors, and an attic. The children had the basement to play in. The rec room, it was called, short for recreation.

"You could keep your eyes peeled when you're doing your rounds, I guess."

"Peeled?"

"Open. Ask the folks you deliver to."

For a moment Tomas felt disappointed. He'd hoped that maybe—well, just *maybe*—Sandy would have said he'd ask his father if the Petersons could come and live with them. But that had been a silly hope, Tomas could see that, now that he thought about it properly. This wasn't wartime, with people doubling up and taking in refugees. Sandy came from a country that had been at war but had not been invaded and occupied. Sandy had always lived in a whole house, just as he himself had done before the war.

First thing in the morning they always had a scripture reading with Miss Lawson, and sang a hymn. This morning Mr. Phillips had come in to join them. He was standing at the front beside Miss Lawson, who looked pink in the face.

73

In spite of the principal's presence, Tomas found he couldn't concentrate. His thoughts kept whirling around. He felt as if the top of his head were about to lift off. What if old Craik were to put them out in the street? He saw Miss Lawson's eyes on him and began opening and shutting his mouth in time with the rest, pretending that he was singing the hymn. The trouble was he didn't know the words, and everyone else seemed to. Something about you in your small corner and I in mine.

They were in a corner all right. The middle of winter, and nowhere to go! His father would die if he were to be put out into the street. In a way, it had been easier to be homeless in Germany; lots of people had been in the same boat. He wouldn't mind living in a boat, a big one that would sail the seven seas. There he was letting his mind go drifting away again.

It was so easy not to latch onto what was happening. For the first three days, when the teacher had asked those who wanted milk to come and get it, he'd gone at once. They were given little bottles of milk and a straw. Each day there had been a bottle short, and somebody had been left without one. It was only after the third day that Tomas realized that you had to *pay* for the milk at the start of the week—at DP camp everything like that had been handed out free—and he'd been doing someone out of his milk. He'd blushed scarlet. He went without milk now; he didn't want to ask his mother for anything extra.

The hymn had stopped, Tomas suddenly realized. Miss Lawson was staring at him. He closed his mouth abruptly. Mr. Phillips now delivered a kind of sermon, in which he talked about duty, to God and the king, whom they were expected to serve and to pray for. (Tomas hoped that serving wouldn't mean fighting, and that no one would start any new wars, as Hugo was eighteen and would be expected to go.) The king was George VI of Great Britain. He was the king for Canada, too, it seemed. Pictures of him and his wife, Queen Elizabeth, and their two daughters, Elizabeth and Margaret Rose, were pinned up on the back wall. And beside the blackboard hung the British flag, which was called a Union Jack. On the other side was the Canadian flag. It was red, with a small Union Jack in the top left-hand corner and a bigger Canadian shield in the bottom right. They'd had to draw both flags in art.

In a place of honor on the back wall there was a picture of the wedding of Princess Elizabeth and somebody called Prince Philip. (No relation to Mr. Phillips!) Tomas wondered if Prince Philip had sent Princess Elizabeth a Valentine card with a heart on it. Miss Lawson seemed very keen on all these people. "Elizabeth and Philip!" she'd say, and her eyes would light up. She'd told them that her grandmother—her grandparents lived in London—had seen the Princess Elizabeth pass by in her glass coach, like a fairy-tale princess on her wedding day. Miss Lawson was proud of that. It was another aspect of life that Tomas was trying to get used to, for it seemed that he, too, was expected to feel proud of this royal family.

Miss Lawson had asked if Latvia had a royal family.

"No, I don't think so."

The class had looked at him as if he had missed out on something. Imagine not having a king and queen!

Mr. Phillips finished his sermon and departed. Suddenly the atmosphere in the classroom changed. The girls started to giggle again. Miss Lawson, who was smiling, said that if anyone had a Valentine card, he or she could put it in the box on her desk; then she'd pick two people to deliver the mail. There was a stampede to put envelopes into the box.

"No pushing now!" cried Miss Lawson.

Tomas was the only one to hang back. He saw himself getting a dirty look from Carol and Helen. The girls, having returned to their desks, were now sitting up very straight, with their arms folded and their eyes fixed on Miss Lawson's, willing her to pick them.

Helen was chosen. She rose, tall and important, from her seat. Carol flicked her pigtails with annoyance and the pink bows bounced. Then a boy named Danny was called on. Helen and Danny were given the box to carry between them, and each in turn picked out an envelope. "Sally!" they called, or "Don!" Sally giggled and hid her face, and Don's ears turned red, and he looked sheepish.

"Carol!"

Carol took the card from Danny's hand, as if she was not really interested. Tomas saw that Sandy's ears had turned pink.

"Love from S," Carol murmured, with a little glance into the row behind. "I wonder who *that* could be!"

"Tom!"

Tomas felt himself getting hot. Helen was bearing down on him with a white envelope. Surely it wasn't for him! Helen was holding it out, her head cocked to one side, a smile on her face. It reminded him of Mrs. Craik's smile. He took the envelope. What else could he do? He didn't look at Sandy.

"Tom!" He heard his name again. And now came Danny with another envelope. He wouldn't tell Astra about all this when he got home. She'd laugh herself silly. Then he remembered Astra was ill and in no laughing mood.

"Open your cards, Tom!" The girl behind him nudged his back.

He did so reluctantly. "From an admirer" said the first one. On the front of the card there were two hearts joined together by two arrows. Someone had written in his initials on one heart and her own on the other. T.P. and A.J. He shrugged.

"A.J.!" shrieked the girl behind him. "Alice Jones! Alice Jones loves you!"

Tomas's face was burning. He didn't look anywhere near where Alice Jones sat. He tore open the second envelope and took out a picture of violets tied with pink ribbon and encircled by a big heart. "Be My Valentine!" it said. Inside there was writing, in pink crayon, decorated with loops and flourishes. "From Guess Who? X." Looking over Carol's half-turned shoulder, Tomas saw a pink crayon sitting in the groove on her desk.

Danny turned the box upside down. It was empty. Sandy hadn't gotten a card from anybody. His face was bright pink, and his bottom lip was pushed out. Tomas opened his desk and shoved his two Valentines inside.

"Just a pleasant little game, children," said Miss Lawson, still smiling. Tomas thought she must have gotten a card from someone. Mr. Phillips? He couldn't imagine the principal writing "I love you" to anyone. "It's an old custom going back to olden times. There were two saints called Valentine, and they're both commemorated on St. Valentine's Day—the fourteenth of February! Do you have that custom in Latvia, Tom?"

"I don't know," he muttered. "Don't think so."

Sandy didn't speak to him for the rest of the day. He went off at recess with Don. Carol didn't speak to him either, but he didn't care about that.

He was glad when school was over for the day. He went straight to the grocer's.

"Hungry, boy?" Mr. Zawacki rummaged in a jar and brought out a cookie.

While they loaded up the basket, Tomas told Mr. Za-wacki that he was looking for an apartment for his family.

"Three rooms, not too much money. Could you help me?"

"How could I help you? I am not in the real estate business! Now you ride steady with all these eggs in the carrier and keep your mind on where you go! I am not wanting scrambled eggs all over the road."

Tomas threw his leg over the bar and eased himself into the seat. The carrier was full almost to overflowing. And now that it was beginning to get dark, the roads would be icing up again. It was a risky business, riding a bike in weather like this.

"You are hearing?"

"Yes, I am hearing."

"But are you listening?"

"Yes, I am listening."

"One minute, then." Tomas put his foot on the curb. Mr. Zawacki was frowning, thinking. "Maybe I do know of an apartment. Mrs. Feinstein say last week she has apartment for let."

"Oh, thanks, Mr. Zawacki!"

There was nothing for Mrs. Feinstein, so Tomas waited until he'd finished the first round of deliveries before calling on her. He was glad to get rid of the last box of eggs without cracking them. The grocer had said that if he broke any, the money would have to come out of his wages. At least with Old Whacky you knew where you were. Half the time Tomas didn't know where he was with the kids at school. They always seemed to know something he didn't know.

Mrs. Feinstein was pleased to see him. She lived alone and had an order delivered weekly. Often she'd give him sweet little honey cakes and ask him in to warm his hands at her stove.

"Ah, Tom! You want to rent my apartment? Yes, it is still free. Come inside, I show you!"

Hugo was mixing concrete. The shovel felt heavy, but not as heavy as it had when he first began on the site. His muscles were building up, and he was learning to work with some sort of rhythm. The work was tedious, though, as well as hard, and he had an uneasy relationship with the men. Or some of them. Most left him alone. Bob was friendly; Kostas, too, of course, but one or two, like Hank, enjoyed having targets to snipe at. Hank liked to get a laugh by making someone else seem foolish. He referred to Hugo and Kostas as the "Deeps." "Let the damn Deeps hang around together!" he'd say.

Hugo got through the tedious parts of the day by letting his mind wander. He'd had a letter from Bettina that morning. Her mother was unwell, and Bettina was worried about her. Bettina had enclosed a photograph of herself taken at Christmas, standing beside the tree, smiling. She was well into her nurses' training now and enjoying it, she said. He had always known she would make a good nurse. When he had lain on the brink of death, she had cared for him well.

At noon, after he had eaten the half loaf of bread that he now brought for his lunch, he had gone to the library and written a letter to Bettina.

"It is all right to write here?" he had asked Irena.

"Of course! As long as you don't make a noise." She had smiled, too. They chatted a little each day, keeping their voices down so as not to disturb the browsers. He had learned that she lived with her mother; her father had died when she was small. Her mother was a seamstress and didn't earn very much. Irena had had to leave school before graduating and take a job. She was taking evening classes and trying to save some money so that she could go to the university one day. She wanted to become a properly qualified librarian.

"What a pity you didn't know about the classes when you came, Hugo! Maybe even now it mightn't be too late."

"My English is not good."

"But math and science—you could do them."

That was true; one need not be fluent in English for those subjects.

"If you could get even one or two credits, it would be a start."

Hugo thought about that conversation while he mixed the concrete. He straightened his back and rested on the spade for a minute. He had told Irena that he did not intend to go to college in Canada, that he planned to return to Germany. But the more he thought about the night classes, the more they seemed a good idea. They would help to keep him up to date and sharpen his mind, which at the moment had nothing more taxing to work on than the consistency of concrete.

He had not told Bettina about these thoughts in his letter; he hadn't wanted to worry her. She knew his father would never be able to work again. She had written, "Your family must need you, Hugo. How can you leave them?"

In his letter he had replied, "Would you not think of coming to Canada, Bettina? Not yet, but once we are on our feet and have a proper place to live . . ."

A proper place! How long would that take to find? He had talked to Irena about trying to find something at a modest rent, and she had said that she would keep her ears open. Sometimes people would tell her they had rooms to let and ask if she knew of anyone looking.

"You could go to an agency, but rents would probably be high. Word of mouth is the best way."

Hugo was about to resume work when he saw Tomas coming whizzing toward him on the grocer's bicycle. The front carrier, which was empty, was bumping up and down. Tomas looked excited.

"Hugo! Hey, *Hugo!*"

"Tom! What is it?"

Tomas leaped from the bicycle, letting it slide down onto the ground, where it lay, its back wheel spinning vigorously.

"I've found us a place, a new place to live! At Mrs. Feinstein's."

"Slow down—and now tell me!"

Tomas gulped for breath. One of his customers, a Mrs. Feinstein, who made fantastic honey cakes, had three rooms to let, for just eighteen dollars.

"That's good," said Hugo cautiously. "What are they like, these rooms?"

"They haven't got much furniture, but we can get some, can't we, from the Salvation Army? The ceilings are not too high, so the rooms would be easy to warm. They're under the eaves, like our rooms at the Frasers'."

"The top floor? How many floors in the house?"

"Three, not counting the basement."

"And the rooms are on the third?"

Tomas was beginning to get the gist of Hugo's questioning. "You don't think they'd be any good?"

"You know Father could never climb two flights of stairs, Tom. We'd have to carry him up, and once he was there, he wouldn't be able to go out."

"How will we ever find anything?" asked Tomas dejectedly, kicking his toe against the curb. "Who's going to let us live on their first floor?"

SEVEN

WHO, INDEED, would rent them rooms on the first floor and at a price they could afford? The question, as the days went by, became pressing. Astra, recovering, but still too weak and tired to go out, had plenty of time to turn it over in her mind.

She studied the apartments and rooms to let in the *Toronto Daily Star*. The furnished apartments were too expensive—a hundred and forty or a hundred and fifty dollars a month. They couldn't possibly afford that. And most of the rooms that would sleep two were ten dollars weekly and had descriptions saying things like "quiet business couple preferred," "refined lady," "business gentlemen, abstainers." Astra doubted if landladies would welcome a family of immigrants that included a child and an invalid father, with the only employed member working on a building site. Hugo could hardly be classed as a business gentleman!

Every day Mrs. Craik, on her way to the laundry room, would stop at their living-room door to inquire if they'd found anything yet. "You'll have to go at the end of the month! I've rented out the rooms, the new people come in on the first." She was not lying. They had seen the people—a couple, man and wife—when she'd shown them around. They had appeared pleased with the accommodation, were not out of the door when the man had said, "We'll take it."

Kristina went to the drugstore and phoned the two old Latvian friends of Ivar Fraser's mother. They had sounded very elderly, she said when she returned. One of them had known Lukas's mother in the days of their youth. They had kept her standing in the phone booth for a long time, reminiscing. "We still miss the old country!" they had said. They had invited the Petersons to come over for a meal one weekend, but they had known of no cheap rooms.

Kristina had then knocked on the doors of the two other houses on their street that had ROOMS TO LET signs in their windows. The houses were decrepit, and the curtains at the windows were torn and filthy, but by this stage they were desperate enough to try anything. In both cases, however, the rooms had been single ones, not for families.

"If worst comes to worst, we shall have to split up," she said.

Astra was sure there must be something suitable for them somewhere; it was just a case of tracking it down. If only she were fit enough to tramp the streets! In Leipzig, when they'd had nowhere to go, it had been she and Mara who found the barn for them to live in.

She'd had another letter from Mara, who seemed to be finding Boston to her liking.

"I have met a nice boy—a Latvian boy, called Janis. And can you imagine, Astra, that he comes from Cesis."

Cesis had been the nearest town to their home in the

country. Astra felt a terrible wave of homesickness engulfing her; and as she read Mara's letter, she wanted, more than anything in the world, to go back home, to the house with the apple green door and the old weathercock on the roof, and the birch wood behind, and the meadow where Klavins' black and white cows grazed. Being closed into this concrete place—this *under*world— with the sound of traffic constantly buzzing, reaching them even here, below ground, made that other world on the edge of the Baltic sea seem green and soft and tranquil. But perhaps it no longer was. Their house might be used to billet Russian soldiers. The cows might have been taken to the slaughterhouse. They had heard that Klavins and his son Valdis had been taken to Siberia—taken because they were farmers. She and Valdis had been sweethearts when they were young!

"Is anything wrong, dear?" Lukas was eyeing her over the top of his book. He spent most of his days reading. When he was a little stronger, he planned to try to get some translating and editing work.

She blinked, recovered. "No, nothing! I was just being silly, that's all. Sentimental. Wishing for something that cannot be."

"We cannot afford to be sentimental," her father said gently. "That would be a luxury."

She nodded.

"We must look forward, Astra."

At once she felt shamed. Here she was, only eighteen years old, and normally in good health, lamenting the past. And there was her father, not so young, frail, unable to work, enclosed by four walls, telling her they must look forward. She went to him and put her arm around his shoulders. He patted her hand.

"Of course we must be allowed some moments in

84

which we can look back, for we don't want to forget who we are or where we come from. We must try to find a balance between the old and the new.''

Feeling better, she got up, saying she would go out for a while.

"Wrap up well! Put on your new coat.''

It was not new—it was fairly shabby, bought cheaply from the Salvation Army—but it was warm and covered her throat. She still had an ache in her breastbone, where she'd frozen it. She pulled on the red boots Shirley had given her and wound a thick scarf over her head and around her neck.

A bitter wind struck her in the face as she climbed up the basement steps. It felt as if it had come straight off the Russian steppes. A few light flakes of snow were spiraling earthward out of the sky. She huddled deep inside her coat, which was so heavy it was weighing down her shoulders. For a moment she despaired that she should still feel so weak. She had gone through all those winters of the war and never been ill. And then she had come to North America, where life, they had heard, would be so much easier, and she had gotten sick! Her thoughts were irrational, she knew. It was not the fault of Canada that she had gotten chilled and succumbed to a virus.

She would scour all the streets in the neighborhood and ask at every house with a ROOMS TO LET sign up. There were not so very many. She had a feeling that she would have no luck, and she did not. At most houses, it was the same story: individual rooms, not family accommodation. None had three rooms vacant. Some did not even answer her knock. She went into a drugstore and called two or three of the numbers in the *Toronto Daily Star* ads, but, as she'd suspected, as soon as she began to describe her family, the landlady's voice turned as chilly as the weather.

She went on walking. She was heading south, toward the lake. After a while she gave up thinking about accommodation. It was good to be outside after being cooped up for so many days in the small room. And it was good to see people going about their ordinary, everyday lives. She walked a long way, came to a yacht club, and then a park beside the lake.

White caps ruffled its gray surface. The expanse of water was great, like a sea. At the edges ice crackled. In summer perhaps they would be able to swim here. Everything would be better once summer came.

Two girls passed her, talking and laughing. They were wrapped up in each other. They did not notice her. She looked after them enviously. She was lonely! She, Astra Petersons, who had never been lonely in her life before. At school she had been popular, a leader, with lots of friends of both sexes. And whoever else had been around, there had always been Mara.

Here she had her family, of course, but Hugo was at work all day, and tired in the evening, or else studying. He'd recently enrolled in night classes in algebra, geometry, and trigonometry, and intended to take the final school examinations in those subjects. He'd seen some examples of previous papers and felt confident about passing. Of course he was brilliant at math. He'd suggested that she take night classes, too, in English and German, but she'd felt too drained to consider it. Now she might, however.

Tomas seemed to be getting to know people on his grocery rounds and at school, although he had come home with some long story about Valentine cards and his friend Sandy not speaking to him. They hadn't quite been able to follow it. But it hadn't sounded like Tomas—being bothered about sending cards with hearts on them to girls! He'd said you were supposed to do it. Kristina had said she found that difficult to believe.

Astra had hoped to go to school herself. She'd have made new friends there. Well, things had not worked out that way. What she needed now—apart from finding a new home for them—was a job.

Tomorrow, she would go in search of one.

Miss Lawson stood in front of the map of the world, with her long wooden pointer.

"Come and show me where Australia is!"

A pupil went forward.

"Scotland! Come and find Scotland, Sandy!"

Sandy went to point to it on the map, where it sat at the top of the British Isles.

"Germany!"

Helen was chosen to find Germany. She ran her finger around its outer boundary, showing how it sat in the center of Europe.

"This map is out of date," said Miss Lawson. "It was made before the war, and the world has changed since then. Germany is now divided into two parts—East and West. Other boundaries in Europe have changed, too. We will have to get new maps. Tom, come and show us where your country is."

Tomas did as he was bid. "This is Latvia. But it is in the Soviet Union now."

"That's right," Miss Lawson said sadly. She was sad for him, he supposed. She probably wouldn't be too bothered herself. His father said nobody cared about the fate of their country, the nations of the West weren't prepared to do anything about it. They didn't want to upset the Soviet leader, Joseph Stalin. They were afraid of starting another world war.

The bell rang, marking the end of the school day. Suddenly a flurry of noise broke out, desk lids went up, bags were packed. A sense of freedom was in the air.

Miss Lawson called to Tomas to stay for a moment. Did she want to speak to him about Latvia? Tell him that she was sorry? He had his bag under his arm, had been about to rush out. He hoped she would not take too long. Usually he was one of the first out the door. He had no time to hang around, not like the others, who straggled across the yard, chewing gum and candy and throwing snowballs. If he was five minutes late, the grocer would grumble, even though Tomas worked until every order was delivered.

The last pupil left the room. Miss Lawson closed the drawer of her desk and locked it. Tomas shifted from one foot to the other.

"You always seem to be in a hurry."

So that was it! He looked down at his feet.

"Do you work after school, Tom?" She asked the question innocently enough, or so it seemed, but Tomas knew at once that she knew. "Look at me, Tom!"

He lifted his head.

"I know, of course, that quite a few children have little jobs. We turn a blind eye to that—as long as they *are* little. Or shall we say that we don't object as long as it doesn't take up too much of their time and tire them out so that they can't do their work at school."

"I do my work at school!"

"I know you do, Tom. You work hard. But you have a lot of catching up to do. There's your English—you should be putting all your energy into that. How many hours a week do you work for Mr. Zawacki?"

"Who told you?"

"I can easily ask him if you won't tell me."

"Twenty," he said heavily.

"Twenty! That's far too many for a boy of your age. No wonder you look tired some mornings. You'll have to cut it down."

"I cannot," he said desperately. "We need money. And Mr. Zawacki would get another boy. Please, Miss Lawson, *please* not to tell Mr. Phillips!"

She sighed. "Oh, all right, Tom! I realize it can't be easy for your family. You have had a tough time. But you must keep up with your work. Do you understand?"

He understood.

He pedaled hard that day, bouncing over the ruts on the road. He wished he could bounce over Sandy's head. He cracked three eggs! Mr. Zawacki was furious, made a note to take it off his wages. In that case," said Tomas, "can I have the cracked eggs for my mother? They are mine if I pay for them."

"Cheeky boy, aren't you?"

"No," said Tomas stubbornly. "It's only fair."

Mr. Zawacki put the eggs into a brown bag. "You are right, young man, to stand up for your rights! No one else is going to do it for you."

Tomas left early for school the next morning. He was one of the first to arrive, but he did not go inside even though it was snowing hard. He stamped his feet and flapped his arms to keep warm. He was waiting for Sandy.

Sandy looked away when Tomas called his name.

"Want to ask you something, Sandy!" He went after him.

"Well?"

"Did you tell Miss Lawson about my job?" Sandy didn't answer. Tomas took hold of his arm. Sandy was smaller and less agile then he was. If it came to a fight, he'd be able to knock him across the yard. His father wouldn't like hear about anything like that! He said fighting solved nothing. Not even between nations. One country might defeat another, but it was not so easy to defeat the hearts and spirits of its people. *"Did* you?" Tomas asked again.

"No, I didn't!"

"I don't believe you!"

"I didn't tell her—not *her.*"

"Who did you tell, then?" Tomas tightened his grip on the other boy's arm. "Who?"

"Carol," said Sandy miserably.

"Carol?" Tomas let go of his arm. "Why?"

"Don't know."

The bell was ringing. They trailed across the yard.

"I didn't mean to," said Sandy.

Tomas thought about it as they tramped along the corridor to their classroom. He sort of knew why Sandy had done it, or thought he did. He'd wanted to get back at him. He'd felt hurt because Carol hadn't sent him a Valentine card. It seemed crazy to Tomas, who had gotten a card from Carol and hadn't wanted it!

"You were right," said Sandy. "That Valentine thing is stupid! My mum said so, too."

At recess, Sandy waited for Tomas. He had two bars of butterscotch in his pocket.

Tomas had never tasted butterscotch before. He liked it.

Astra studied the employment column in the newspaper. There were a number of ads for cleaning ladies and baby-sitters but she was wary about those after her experience with Shirley. She marked a couple of others and set out.

The first place she tried was a dog food factory. The personnel officer was pleasant and put her at ease. He complimented her on her English. There were many refugees working in the factory, he told her. Poles, Czechs, Ukrainians. "You name them, we've got them!" The pay was sixty-seven cents an hour, forty-four hours a week.

"How does that sound to you?"

"It sounds fine."

"I think you'd suit us. You look fit enough."

"Oh I am, very fit." She had rubbed a little rouge onto her cheeks before coming out. Shirley had given her some half-used makeup one day when she was clearing out the drawers in her bedroom.

"Can you start right away? Tomorrow?"

She nodded. It seemed she had a job, a paying one, just like that!

"Come and I'll show you around the factory, then!"

She followed him out of his office along a corridor. He opened a door. Immediately, her senses were assaulted—her ears with the noise of machines and her nose with the odor of cooking dog food. It was the smell that was so overwhelming. She had never smelled anything so revolting. Perhaps, in time, she would get used to it. She followed the personnel officer between the bubbling cauldrons of meat, which must come from the leftovers of all the animal carcasses considered unfit for human beings. Nausea rose up from her stomach into her throat. She fought hard to control it. She put a hand to her mouth, gagged, and brought up the remains of her half-digested breakfast on the floor.

Back outside some minutes later, she felt grateful for the sharp, cutting wind that was sweeping the street. Even the unsavory meals in refugee camps had not turned her stomach in such a way. The personnel officer had said perhaps the job would not suit her after all and reluctantly, she had had to agree. The money would have been good, but not the smells.

The next place on her list was a dry cleaner's on College Street. Her mother had advised against that, had said the cleaning fluids would not be good for her lungs. But she was beginning to feel desperate. She had to find some way to earn money, and nothing she could get would be ideal.

The dry cleaner's was nearer home, within walking distance. That would be one advantage. Though where "home" would be in three days' time, she was not sure. It seemed that they might have to take separate rooms, at least in the meantime. They'd found one big one and a small one in a house that would do for her parents and Tomas, and two small rooms in another street for herself and Hugo.

A girl about her own age stood behind the counter, taking clothes from the customers and writing out tickets. That was a job that Astra would not mind. No smells, and people to talk to. The woman checking in her laundry now was from some country in the Far East. She seemed to speak no English. The man behind her sounded central European.

Astra waited until the girl at the counter was free.

"Hi! Can I help you?"

"I've come about the job."

"Oh, okay! I'll go and get Mrs. Glegg—she's the manager."

Mrs. Glegg had white-blonde hair, piled high, and walked on heels so tall that she seemed in danger of toppling over. She looked Astra up and down.

"Any experience?"

"No, but I am willing to learn. I am quick to learn."

"Vacancy's for a trouser presser."

Astra nodded, uncertain what that would mean. "I can iron," she volunteered.

"You don't have to be good at ironing. Come through and I'll show you."

The counter girl gave Astra an encouraging grin as she moved off in the wake of the manager. The back premises were hot and steamy and smelled of chemicals—cleaning fluid, Astra presumed. She could feel herself beginning to sweat under her heavy serge coat. She undid the buttons.

Some women were tending machines, others folding and arranging clothes over hangers. All were middle-aged. Their faces were tired; their shoulders drooped. The manager stopped in front of the trouser-pressing machine. It consisted of two boards, one on the top and one on the bottom. She lifted a pair of trousers and laid the legs over the bottom board. Then she put her foot on a pedal, and the top board came down. There was a hiss of steam. She stepped on another pedal, and the top board came up. The bottom half of the trousers was now pressed.

"That's all there is to it."

"That's all?"

"Someone else does the top part—that's the harder part. Ella over there does that."

Ella was wearing slippers, and her feet looked swollen.

"Think you can manage it?"

Astra nodded. She knew that it would be a job that would bore her rigid. Probably literally, after she'd stood there for eight hours in one spot working two pedals. But it was a job.

"Sixty cents an hour," said the manager.

"Sixty!"

"That's the rate."

Astra hesitated—it was less than the dog food factory, but at least the smells wouldn't make her sick. Then she said, "Okay, I'll take it."

That evening, she went with Hugo to his night school. Her father had repeated what she already knew: There was only one way to make sure that she would not have to go on doing boring jobs like cooking dog meat or pressing trousers. She asked the principal if she could enroll for German classes and also for English language and literature.

"We're halfway through the year."

"I know. But I speak German fluently, and I have read a great deal in English."

Lukas had also told her that she must present herself boldly and confidently.

She was accepted.

Astra enjoyed the two hours of English literature. It was such a relief to put her mind to something interesting and absorbing, like the plays of Shakespeare, instead of the constant worrying about a place to live and lack of money.

When she came out of the classroom, she saw Hugo talking to a girl in the corridor. He called to her.

"Astra, come here!"

She went.

"This is Irena. Irena, my sister Astra."

The girls shook hands. They eyed each other. Astra saw a small, slim girl with blonde hair braided around her head. She knew that Irena was the girl from the library. Was Hugo interested in her? But he was engaged to Bettina, wrote faithfully to her twice a week, received regular letters back.

Astra had an instinctive feeling that Irena was not going to be friendly to her. There was a coolness in her glance. But perhaps there was in hers, too. She must try to be fair!

"Irena is offering us a place to live! In her house."

"In *her* house?" Astra turned from Hugo to Irena.

"My mother lets rooms, and, just today, one of our tenants has had to leave suddenly."

"But there are five of us."

"He had two rooms. And my mother can offer another one."

It seemed a marvelous opportunity, yet Astra felt reluctant to take it. She was being silly, she told herself. She must not make such rash judgments about this girl. Irena had taken an interest in Hugo, helped him, encouraged him to join the night school. Perhaps that was it: *She* was interested in Hugo. And Astra might be someone who would get in the way. Astra doubted that Hugo would realize any of this; he tended to be happily unaware of what people were feeling toward him—especially if that person was a girl. Mara had been soft on him for a long time, but he had not known it.

Irena invited them to come home with her and inspect the rooms for themselves.

She lived only a few streets away from Mrs. Craik's house. The two rooms that the tenant had had were on the top floor. Alongside them were a small kitchenette and a bathroom. Irena and her mother, Mrs. Simmonds, occupied the second floor and part of the first. In the basement lived another lodger. Irena had told Hugo that it was only by having lodgers that they were able to buy the house. The rents they received paid their mortgage. Many immigrants bought houses this way.

"I can let your parents have this room," said Mrs. Simmonds, opening a door on the ground floor.

The room was large but unfurnished. Furniture would not be a problem; the Salvation Army was a good source of cheap goods. Some things you could get for nothing, but ten dollars should buy a decent table, said Mrs. Simmonds. Or they could try the Scott Mission on Spadina, run by the Reverend Zeidman. The room would easily be able to serve as a bedroom for Kristina and Lukas and as a family living room.

"Irena says the rooms are light," said Hugo, whose mind was made up, Astra saw.

The rent was twenty-five dollars a week. They might just be able to manage it.

"We'll have to discuss it with out parents," said Astra.

"Of course," said Mrs. Simmonds.

There was really nothing to discuss. In the morning Astra and Kristina went to the Simmonds' and paid a week's rent in advance, money that Kristina had put aside from Tomas's earnings. They moved in the next day.

EIGHT

"OUR NEW LODGINGS are very much better," Hugo wrote to Bettina, in the small pool of light cast by the table lamp. He had a blanket draped around his shoulders. It was cold up here under the roof; there was a radiator, but it was a long way from the basement furnace, and it was never more than luke-warm. In the bed against the wall Tomas lay asleep, one arm flung above his head. The wall was plastered with cutouts of cars—Cadillacs, Chryslers, Lincolns, Hudsons, Packards, Buicks. Hugo could not remember all the names. Tomas could, though; he was car mad. He cut the pictures from magazines scrounged from customers or picked out of garbage cans, and stuck them to the wall with green Palmolive soap.

Hugo pushed up his glasses, rubbed his eyes. They felt tired and gritty, as he did. He had been up since six-thirty, had worked all day on the site, and had gone to algebra class in the evening. The symbols had been dancing in front of his eyes by the time the final bell rang. He thought he might need new glasses, but since he couldn't afford them, he'd have to make do with these in the meantime.

The first brand-new thing they planned to buy was a coat for their father. It was his birthday at the beginning of April, and his only coat was ragged and thin. He should soon be able to go for short walks. They wanted him to be able to step out smartly dressed.

Hugo and Astra had been to Eaton's department store and picked out a coat. It cost sixty-five dollars. To them that was a lot of money. They had hesitated a long time. They could buy it on credit, the assistant had told them, pay for it bit by bit. After further consultation, they had put down a deposit. The coat was tweed, a rich brown flecked with black. The buttons were covered with leather. They knew that their father would like such a coat. Fingering the material, they smiled, imagining him pulling it on, settling it on his shoulders. Before the war he had taken pride in being well-dressed.

Hugo picked up his pen again. He wanted to go to bed, to sleep, but he had not written to Bettina for several days. He had so little time left over after working and studying. He must write tonight. She would worry if she did not hear from him.

"It is good not to have to live in a basement any more," he wrote. He wrote in German. The only time that he thought in German now was when he wrote to Bettina. The language was being pushed to the back of his mind, when for four years, it had been the only language that he had spoken. "We hated being below ground level. And it is good not to have to tolerate a woman like Mrs. Craik. She was very nasty to us when we were leaving, and tried to make us pay for 'damages.' She said we had chipped her light shade, dented her kettle, and cracked her sink! All of these things were like that when we moved in. Father was polite to her, but he told her quite firmly that we had not damaged anything. He has written now to put the record straight with Mr. Fraser. Mr. and Mrs. Fraser were very upset.

"Our new landlady, Mrs. Simmonds, is much nicer. She welcomed us warmly when we arrived and insisted that we take our first meal in the house with her family. She is Estonian, from Tallin, and we feel at home with her. She understands what it is like to be immigrants in a strange country."

Hugo paused with the pen over the paper. What else did he have to tell Bettina? She would not want to hear about the problems he had solved in algebra that evening. And she did not know the men he worked with, so he could not expect her to be interested in them.

"I must go to bed now, Bettina," he finished. "It is late, and I have to leave early for work, as you know. Mother and Father send their best wishes, as does Astra. With fondest love, Hugo."

In the adjoining room sat Astra, also writing a letter—hunched, too, under a blanket, her fingers stiff with cold. She was writing to Mara, in Latvian. And in spite of the cold, she was writing fast.

"Our new landlady is good and kind and doesn't look at us as if we'd crawled out of some hole. It's a change! I am not so sure about her daughter, Irena. She *seems* pleasant enough but I think she's more pleasant to everyone else in the family than to me. She's very sweet to Father. 'Let me help you, Professor Petersons! Can I fetch you anything?' I find her too sweet. Are you thinking I am being hard on her, Mara? Maybe I am.

"You see, I think she fancies Hugo. In fact, I am certain she does. She can't take her eyes off him. And great

99

big lump that he is, he doesn't even realize it. He never sees what's going on under his nose. He has it stuck in a math book most of the time, anyway. And you know how he is with girls! He is a sitting target for any girl who wants to manipulate him. Well, how else do you think he got betrothed to Bettina? At his age! It's crazy. She must have been the one to want it. Can you imagine him ever *thinking* about getting married? Bettina is a very nice girl, though, I have to admit—genuinely nice. Nicer than Irena! Bettina could make Hugo a very good wife, when he is ready. Which will not be for years and years. But I am sure Bettina will never leave Germany and her parents. They were all so good to Hugo, saving his life, keeping him alive, that he feels indebted to them. Who wouldn't? But can he feel under that obligation forever? It is a big problem for Hugo.

"Oh, Mara, I wish you were here, so that we could talk and talk! There is no one else I can say these things to. Mother cuts me off if I criticize Irena. She says I am too quick to make judgments, and if it weren't for Irena, we would all be split up and living in horrible rooming houses.

"I have started work at a dry cleaner's. I press trouser bottoms! I stand there all day long doing just that. Sometimes, if we are not busy, I get to put cardboard covers over wire coat hangers. Can you see me? You know I am not famous for my patience! But at work I am patient. I have to be.

"Most of the women are married, with half a dozen kids, and struggling to make ends meet. You can see the struggle on their faces. Now, Mara, if you marry this Janis, you must *not* have six children. (Are you blushing?) Because if you do, you will spend your life bowed down with burdens.

"There is one girl my age at the cleaner's—Nancy, who works at the counter. She's seventeen, and she comes to work all dressed up as if she were going to a dance. High-heeled shoes with ankle straps and fan-pleated skirts and lipstick and earrings that jingle like a gypsy's. She thinks I am very old-fashioned because my skirts are above the knee and my jacket has shoulder pads. She says you can spot a European a mile off! She says we are all behind the times. We look like people in wartime movies. She would like to reform me. We shall see!

"Now that Father can be left alone during the day, Mother has taken a job house cleaning." Astra paused. She had been going to say that they had not wanted her to take it, that they thought the work too hard for her—and yes, that *she* should not have to clean for other people—when she remembered that Olga, Mara's mother, had cleaned for them in the old days in Latvia, and worked now as a school cleaner. Kristina had said that she was not too proud to do cleaning work. Why should she be? They were poor. Times had changed for them.

Astra bent her head once more to her letter.

"When will I ever see you again, Mara? Don't you often wish you could find a hundred-dollar bill dropped in the street? If I do find one, I will come and visit you in Boston. Write *soon!*

"Love to everyone, Astra."

A hundred-dollar bill. It was a pleasant thought. But if she *were* to find one, there would be many things to spend it on other than a ticket to Boston. But she longed so much to see Mara again.

"A place of meeting," Miss Lawson wrote on the black-board with a new stick of squeaking chalk, which made

101

their nerves squeak too. "That is what the name Toronto means," she said, laying down the chalk and wiping her hands on the sides of her skirt. "And it is very true especially now, with people coming and meeting here from all over the world."

Tomas had his eyes on Carol's pigtails, which today were sporting yellow ribbons.

"The name Toronto is of Huron Indian origin. The original site of the city was at the southern end of the main Indian trails connecting Lake Huron and Lake Ontario." Miss Lawson took her long ruler and showed them on the map. "Tom, are you paying attention?"

Tomas started guiltily. "Yes, Miss Lawson."

"What does the name Toronto mean?"

"Meeting," whispered Sandy.

"Meeting," repeated Tomas.

"Place," whispered Sandy.

"Place," said Tomas.

In front, Carol tried to turn her head. Her shoulders jerked, the pigtails did not move.

Miss Lawson eyed Tomas, then returned to her theme. "Three hundred years ago the site was covered with thick, dense forest . . ."

Carol made another attempt to flick her braids, and let out a sharp squeal. She grasped the back of her head with her hands. Now she screamed.

Miss Lawson came striding down the aisle to see what was going on. Everyone in the rows behind Carol was giggling.

"My pigtails are tied to the desk," sobbed Carol. "It hurts, Miss Lawson, it hurts!"

"Stop screaming, child, and be still for a minute!" Miss Lawson untied the string and released the twists of hair. Then she turned to Tomas.

"Did *you* do this, Tom Petersons?"

Tomas nodded.

"I am surprised at you! Leave the room at once and stand outside the door!"

Tomas slunk out, his head down, and closed the door behind him. He knew that Miss Lawson thought Mr. Phillips would come by and ask him what he was doing standing there. He would then give him a terrible talking to. Perhaps he would even give him the strap.

He flattened himself against the wall, as if to make himself less visible. A murmur came from his own classroom and from the others off the corridor. He had been threatening to tie Carol's pigtails together for a long time. Sandy and Don had dared him to do it, and he had! It served Carol right! Hadn't she told on him for working at Mr. Zawacki's? He didn't even care if Mr. Phillips did strap him—though he hoped that he would not. For one thing, he didn't want Carol to have the chance to crow over him.

He didn't want to get detention that afternoon, either. Because of his job, he couldn't afford to be kept at school late. And he wanted to be home as early as possible, for tonight was a special night. It was his father's birthday. Perhaps he should have thought of that when he tied Carol's pigtails together, but he hadn't. They were having a special birthday meal, and Astra was going to Eaton's to pick up the coat. They were all excited about the coat. Wait till their father saw it!

Shifting from one foot to the other, Tomas felt his arms and legs getting restless. He had never found it easy to stand still. They were having PE later, and he hoped that Miss Lawson would not keep him from going and make him do sums in the classroom instead. She knew how much he loved athletics and sports, especially basketball. He was the best shot in the class.

He stiffened, hearing a noise at the other end of the

corridor. Footsteps were coming his way—heavy footsteps.

As Mr. Phillips turned the corner, Tomas launched himself off the wall and walked toward him.

"Where are you off to, Tom?"

"The washroom, sir."

"Don't be long then!"

"No, sir."

"You seem to be settling in all right?"

"Yes, sir."

Tomas hung around for five minutes or so in the lavatory, washing his hands laboriously, keeping the water running in the basin.

Returning slowly along the corridor, he took up his position again. If Mr. Phillips were to come back this way, he would have no new excuses to make.

The door of Room 7 opened, and out came Miss Lawson. "Perhaps you've had long enough to cool your heels and regret what you've done?" she said.

"Yes, Miss Lawson."

"You may come in now."

He followed her in.

"And what do you have to say to Carol?"

"I'm sorry, Carol," he mumbled, not quite looking her in the eye.

Sitting down, he raised his thumb to Sandy and Don, and grinned.

At lunchtime Hugo went to the library as usual. Irena was at the desk. They talked in whispers.

"Mother has baked a special almond cake with frosted icing for your father. I helped to ice it last night. It is to be a surprise."

"He is going to have lots of surprises!"

104

"I hope the coat fits."

"Oh yes, it will. I tried it on. Father is about my size, a bit thinner, but the same across the shoulders."

A woman in a blue knitted hat, reading at a table, looked over at them and frowned. Hugo nodded at Irena and went off to find a seat. How kind it was of Irena and her mother to make a cake for their father! They must invite them to join the family for Lukas's birthday dinner.

"Thank goodness it's a half day!" said Nancy, as she combed her hair in front of the mirror in the little back room used by the staff. There was space in it for no more than two people at a time. All the other women had left, rushing off with their shopping bags, heading for the grocery stores to buy food for their families.

"Are you going downtown?" asked Astra, buttoning her coat. "I'll walk with you. I'm going to Eaton's to pick up my father's coat."

"Oh, okay! Say, how do you like my new skirt?" Nancy lifted up the hem on both sides and held the skirt out at waist level. "It's a complete circle, do you see? It's called a ballerina skirt. You could make yourself one, Astra. I'll help you."

"It would need a lot of material."

"Why don't you treat yourself just this once? You shouldn't be wearing such dowdy clothes at your age!"

"Maybe I'll make one sometime. Not now. We have to pay for Father's coat first."

"When you do, I'm going to take you dancing at the Palace Pier—that's a promise!"

It sounded more like a threat to Astra, who was not at all sure that she would enjoy such an outing.

The girls walked downtown together, with Nancy

stopping every few yards to look in the store windows. There was nothing that she did not seem to want.

"Wouldn't you like some nice things too?"

"Of course! And I will have them—one day."

They parted outside Eaton's, and Astra went in. She paid off the last installment on the coat. She, Hugo, and their mother had each been contributing to it weekly from their pay.

"It's a lovely coat," said the assistant, as she folded it in tissue paper.

Astra called for her mother on the way home. Kristina worked for a Mrs. Martin, who lived in a big house not far from Mike and Shirley. Kristina was ironing in the kitchen when Astra arrived.

"Have you got the coat?"

Astra held the box aloft.

"Good. I won't be long, love. I've just got one or two pillow cases left to do." Kristina put down the iron and rested a moment, putting a hand to the small of her back. She looked weary, though she denied it when Astra said so. Astra felt a pang at seeing her mother slaving over someone else's ironing.

But Kristina liked Mrs. Martin and said she was no slave driver. They had coffee and a sandwich together at lunchtime and talked, about their families mostly.

Mrs. Martin came in now and was introduced to Astra. She was carrying some clothes over her arm.

"Maybe you'd like to try them on, dear? They're from my daughter Sally—she's a bit older than you, but about your size."

There was a cream-colored raincoat, a skirt in a lovely cornflower blue, and a white blouse with a little collar and a black ribbon bow.

"It's called a little boy collar," Mrs. Martin explained.

"That's very kind of you, Mrs. Martin," said Kristina. "Why don't you put them on, Astra?"

The skirt was in the ballerina style, with four gored pieces to make a circle, just like the one that Nancy wore. Both the skirt and the blouse fitted Astra perfectly. The skirt came down to her mid-calf. Mrs. Martin stepped back admiringly.

"You look lovely, dear!"

"Thank you, Mrs. Martin."

Astra laughed and spun around, so that the skirt swished against her legs. It made her feel good to put on some pretty clothes. Now she would have something new to wear for Lukas's party. And the raincoat, too, felt nice to wear. She tightened the belt, put up the collar, stuck her hands in the pockets. In this coat she could go places that she could not go in the Salvation Army one.

"Leave the rest of the ironing for now, Mrs. Petersons," said Mrs. Martin, "and be on your way. I know it's a big evening for you."

When they got home, Astra smuggled the coat up the stairs into her room. Lukas was resting in the living room. She then went down to help her mother prepare the meal. They were having roast pork—a big treat!

Hugo arrived home soon afterward. He did not seem to notice Astra's new outfit. He had something else on his mind. He said, "We must invite Mrs. Simmonds and Irena to Father's dinner."

"Why must we?" demanded Astra. "This is our family party."

"They've made Father a fine cake."

"In that case—" said Kristina.

"I don't see why we should. After all, we didn't *ask* them to make it."

107

"Come on now, Astra," chided her mother, "they have been generous to us. We must be generous in return. I shall go and invite them now."

"You should watch that Irena!" said Astra, when their mother had gone.

Hugo frowned. "What do you mean—*watch* her?"

"Oh, nothing!"

"Why are you in a bad mood?"

"I'm not!"

She had to go up to her room and take a few deep breaths. Before they had been separated, she and Hugo had always been able to read what was on the other's mind. She still felt that she could read *his* mind, but he seemed no longer able to read hers. Perhaps it was because they were older. Were they growing apart? No, that could not be! She put the idea out of her head.

By the time they were ready to set the food on the table, Astra had recovered her equilibrium. She would not spoil her father's birthday.

He complimented her on her appearance. "That color suits you, Astra." It made her eyes seem more blue. In other lights, wearing other colors, they looked quite gray.

"I am very fond of blue," said Irena, who was wearing a dress of that color herself, with a little string of pearls around her neck and pearl studs in her ears. She looked very demure sitting there with her hands folded in her lap. Immediately Astra wished that her own skirt was scarlet. How foolish she was being!

After the meal, they gave Lukas his presents. Mrs. Simmonds and Irena had bought him a pair of fur-lined, leather gloves.

"They are the most beautiful gloves I have ever seen. This is too generous of you!"

"Try them on, Professor Petersons!" Irena begged.

They fitted perfectly.

"We have something to go with the gloves, Lukas." Kristina was smiling. "Fetch the parcel, Astra!"

Astra went to get it. When she brought it in, Lukas said, "What *have* you been buying? I hope you have not been spending too much money on me?"

"*Priecīgu dzimšnas dienu!*" Happy birthday! she said, and kissed him. "From all of us."

"Open it, Papa!" cried Tomas. "Open it!"

Patiently Lukas undid the string, which he then passed to Kristina to wind over her fingers into a small skein. She would lay it aside in a drawer for further use. They wasted nothing that came into the house, a legacy from their days in the camps. Now he opened up the brown paper wrapping, and when he saw the coat lying there neatly folded in the tissue paper, he was too astonished to speak. He touched the cloth with his fingertips and shook his head wonderingly. Tomas clapped his hands and burst out laughing.

"Try it on, Papa!"

They all stood up for the trying-on of the coat. Tomas danced around on his toes like a boxer in the ring. Astra and Hugo helped ease their father's arms into the sleeves. Kristina did up the leather buttons and smoothed the material across his chest. She kept her hands on his shoulders and looked up at him. Her eyes were shining. He straightened his back.

"How do I look?"

"Like a very fine gentleman," said Irena quickly, and Astra glanced at her with annoyance. How dare she intrude at this very special moment!

"Thank you, Irena." Lukas bowed. "I feel like I am a millionaire. Because I have such a marvelous family!"

* * *

109

He went walking two or three days later, wearing his handsome tweed coat and his leather gloves, and carrying the walking stick that Hugo had bought at the Salvation Army store. The day was much milder than usual. The snow was almost cleared from the backyards; only the hard-packed patches remained. Mrs. Simmonds said that the weather at this time of year could be deceptive; it could turn mild and then go back to winter in one fell swoop. But spring was more or less here, she agreed; the worst of the cold weather was behind them.

He went as far as the dry cleaner's and stopped off to show himself to Astra. The manager was not pleased when Astra left her pressing machine to go and speak to him.

"Just one minute, Mrs. Glegg, *please!* It's so important to him—you can have no idea."

And Mrs. Glegg *could* have no idea, Astra thought, as she dodged around the women putting clothes on hangers; she could not be expected to understand. The coat had a special meaning for him, and for them: It symbolized a brand-new start, a recovery from his illness. Wearing it, he could go out into the world again. And the buying of it showed that they could make their way here if they worked hard.

"You look swell, Mr. Petersons," Nancy was telling Lukas. "It's a great coat."

"A great coat for a great man," said Astra, bringing a twinkle into his eyes.

From there he went to Zawacki's store and talked a while with the grocer. He was pleased to be making the acquaintance of all these people whom his children talked about and who were now a part of their lives. Then he sought out the building site, but he was only able to wave to Hugo, as Hugo was mixing concrete with a noisy machine that could not be abandoned. But he saw Bob, the man in the plaid jacket, and he picked out Kostas, the Lithuanian.

His next stop was the library. Irena was pleased to see him. She came out from behind the counter to greet him.

"Shall I find you a seat, Professor Petersons?"

"No, Irena, I'm not ready yet for sitting. I've done enough of that recently. I was thinking I might like to go and take the air in a park. Can you suggest one?"

Kristina arrived home to find their rooms empty. Lukas's coat was missing. He must have gone for a walk. She hoped he would not stay out too long and overtax himself.

He had still not returned by the time Hugo and Astra came in. Daylight was dwindling fast, and although the sun had been shining earlier, it had gone in now, and gray clouds threatened rain.

"Don't worry, Mother," said Hugo. "I'm sure he will be all right. He looked fine when I saw him earlier."

The back door opened, and in came Irena, home from the library.

"Have you seen our father by any chance?" asked Hugo.

Irena told them that he had gone to High Park, which was about three miles away.

"I hope he hasn't gotten lost," said Astra.

"I don't see how he could. I told him to take the streetcar along Bloor and get off at High Park. He could always ask the way. It's not as if he doesn't speak English."

Another hour passed. It was dark outside. By now they were all concerned, the Simmonds also. They gathered in the kitchen.

"What if he has collapsed somewhere?" said Kristina.

"Perhaps I should have tried to dissuade him." Irena was distressed. "But he said he wasn't tired."

"It's not your fault, Irena," said Hugo.

"I'm going to look for him." Astra pulled on the raincoat that Mrs. Martin had given her.

"I'll come with you."

As Hugo was about to go for his jacket, they heard something outside. They cocked their heads. It sounded like shuffling feet. Swiftly Astra moved to the door and opened it. Then she took a step back.

"*Father!*"

"What is it?" asked Hugo.

Lukas was standing on the porch, leaning on his stick. And from him was coming the most dreadful smell, one that they had never encountered before. It was a suffocating, acrid smell. Astra put her hands over her face.

"I was walking in the park," he said, "and some animal ran in front of me. Black and white, I think it was. I couldn't see properly, it was almost dark. Perhaps it was a cat. It was then that the smell came."

"Skunk!" cried Mrs. Simmonds, horrified. "It must have sprayed your coat, Professor Petersons."

NINE

"NO, PROFESSOR PETERSONS, please don't come inside!" said Mrs. Simmonds, as Lukas started to come into the kitchen. "The stench will fill the house for weeks. It is a terrible thing to get rid of."

He stood on the porch, looking helpless, holding his hand over the lower part of his face. The smell was nearly choking him, and his eyes were streaming. They all felt helpless. Kristina had gone to fetch a bottle of eau de cologne that a friend had given them as a farewell present in Esslingen. She threw some of the contents over the coat, and the odor of cheap perfume mingled with that of skunk, but did not mask it.

"The mild day must have tempted the skunk out," said Mrs. Simmonds. "They hibernate in winter."

"I'd no idea there would be *wild* animals in parks," said Lukas.

Astra appealed to Mrs. Simmonds. "What should Father do? He can't stand there all night."

Their landlady took charge. "Take off the coat, Professor Petersons. Leave it on the step. Now your trousers. And your shoes. They may have been sprayed too."

Stripped of his fine new coat and his trousers, clad only in shirt and long johns, and in his stockinged feet, Lukas was at last permitted to come inside. Mrs. Simmonds closed the door decisively, shutting out the smell, though not totally. Traces of it lingered around Lukas, around all of them. Astra, sniffing the sleeve of her raincoat, thought she could detect it there. She pulled a lock of her hair across her face. That also smelled.

"What are we to do about the coat, Mrs. Simmonds?" asked Kristina. "We can't throw it away."

"We had a dog once that got sprayed by a skunk. We washed her in tomato juice."

"Tomato juice!" Astra was horrified. Imagine dipping their father's beautiful new tweed coat in tomato juice! "Couldn't I take it to my dry cleaner's?"

"They would never let it into the shop as it is, stinking of skunk. It would make everything in the place smell."

"Let me get you a cup of coffee, Lukas," said Kristina. "We'll go into the living room. You look exhausted."

"I had to walk back from High Park."

"You had to *walk*?"

"The driver wouldn't let me get on the streetcar."

"Poor Papa!" said Astra.

Kristina led him away. Astra filled the kettle. What *were* they to do with the coat? Some symbol it was turning out to be—only one day old and contaminated by a skunk!

"Isn't there *anything* else we can do, Mrs. Simmonds?"

"If the coat were mine, I think I'd throw it away. But I believe when the spray dries, it coagulates into small blobs that can then be picked off. It would be a terrible job, though."

114

Not so terrible as throwing the coat away.

Mrs. Simmonds took out a bottle of ammonia and uncorked it. The pungent odor of *that* now filled the kitchen. "We must try to drown the smell somehow."

"We are very sorry," said Hugo.

"It's nobody's fault, Hugo. These things happen." Mrs. Simmonds left them in the kitchen.

Astra reopened the back door. There, on the step, lay the coat in a sad heap. She had to shut the door again quickly.

"We shall have to try to pick off the bits," said Hugo.

After work the next day, they tackled it. They each wore old nylon overalls that Mrs. Simmonds had unearthed from the basement and rubber gloves, and they were armed with tweezers. They sat on the porch floor with the coat between them. The skunk's spray had gone in a wide arc across the front, just above the hemline. The coat had certainly lost its brand-new look. Astra wanted to weep!

"After we've picked all these off, I shall take it to work and get it dry-cleaned."

"Then it will be as good as new."

She gave Hugo a bleak smile. At times it became difficult to be persistently cheerful in the face of setbacks. They had survived the last five years by being determined not to be defeated. Their parents had kept the family buoyed up, and they seldom allowed their children to see them despairing. Yet, often they must have felt on the brink of despair—when they'd had to abandon their home, when Hugo had gotten lost, when they'd been close to starvation at the end of the war. It was no wonder that Lukas's heart was affected.

At least the weather was encouraging. The mild spell was continuing, making life on the construction site a little easier for Hugo. In the backyards the daffodils were beginning to bloom. Soon it would be Easter, and Good Friday would be a holiday from work.

They continued picking off the blobs, putting them carefully into an old newspaper, until darkness drove them in. They resumed their chore the next evening. And then the job was finished.

Astra took the coat to be cleaned the next day. It still smelled a little, but Mrs. Glegg allowed it to come into the shop. When it emerged from the dry-cleaning machine, it *did* look almost new again. Tears of relief came into Astra's eyes.

She packed it up after work. Everyone else had gone except for the manager, who was sitting in a chair with her shoes kicked off and her feet on a shelf. She was smoking a long American cigarette.

"Murder on the feet, this job." She yawned. "So're you liking Toronto?"

"It's okay. It takes a while to get used to a new place."

"I guess it must. You'll be looking forward to Easter. Not going away, are you?"

"Oh no, we couldn't afford to. We're trying to save as much money as possible so that we can have a house of our own one day. Are you going away?" asked Astra politely.

"We're going to Boston to visit my husband's brother."

"To *Boston?*"

"Know it?"

"No. But I would *love* to go to Boston." Astra told her about their friends the Jansons. "They're like family to us."

"Johnny and I could give you a lift to Boston for the weekend if you'd like."

Astra stared at her. Mrs. Glegg had spoken casually, as if she were doing no more than offering a lift to the end of the road. Did she *really* mean she could take her to Boston with them? Astra could not believe it. The very idea made her tremble with excitement.

"We've got a small van. It wouldn't be very comfortable in the back, but you're welcome to bed down in it. We're going to travel overnight on Thursday, being that the store will be closed Good Friday. And the other girls can take care of it on Saturday. We're thinking of taking Monday off as well, to make it a good long weekend. It's quite a way to Boston, you know. We reckon on fifteen hours."

"Don't you need a visa for the U.S.?"

Mrs. Glegg shook her head. "You've got Canadian papers, haven't you? We can go in and out of the U.S. any time we want. It's no problem, I tell you."

"Father, Mrs. Glegg says it's all right," said Astra anxiously. When she had come running in with her news, Lukas had turned the idea down right away. He was uneasy about her crossing the border into another country when she was not a citizen of this one. An apprehension about borders was part of their refugee inheritance.

"I'm sure you must need a visa."

"Mrs. Glegg says it's all right as long as you've got Canadian papers. Please, Father, *please* let me go! I'll never get another chance like this to see Mara. You know how I miss her."

"The worst that could happen, Lukas," said Kristina, "would be that she would be turned back at the border. As long as she has enough money to get home, there's no need to worry."

117

"I suppose that is true," Lukas admitted grudgingly.

"I can go then." Astra flung her arms around him. Her eyes were shining. She went at once to write to Mara.

When Tomas heard that Astra was going to visit the Jansons, he was furious.

"You're going to *Boston* next week? You'll see Zigi! Ask them to take me, too, Astra, ask them, *please!* I couldn't bear it if you went and I didn't."

But Lukas said absolutely not. He would not allow it.

"It's not fair!"

"Possibly not." Their father, however, would not change his mind. "I shall not be happy until Astra returns. I don't want to have to worry about two of you."

Mrs. Glegg decided that she and Astra could leave for Boston early Thursday afternoon. Her husband, Johnny, came to pick them up at the dry cleaner's. He was a big man with thick black hair and a heavy mustache. He was a long-distance truck driver, drove all over the province of Ontario. Driving to Boston and back for a long weekend was no sweat for him, said his wife. He enjoyed driving.

Nancy came out to the sidewalk to wave them off.

"Have a good time!" she yelled, as Johnny revved up the engine.

Astra waved to Nancy out of the back window. Johnny pulled into the stream of traffic, and they were away—to Boston and the Jansons!

They stopped at a roadside cafe just short of the U.S. border and had hot dogs and coffee. "Can't be very comfortable in the back," observed Mrs. Glegg, or Gloria, as she had told Astra to call her.

118

"I'm fine. I've ridden in worse, much worse. Coal wagons, without a roof."

"Coal wagons? On the railroad? You haven't!"

Astra told them a little about their journey through southern Germany at the end of the war, when they'd been shunted from camp to camp. "Nobody knew what to do with us. There were ten million or so homeless in Germany alone, from countries all over Europe—eastern Europe mostly."

"The things you kids have had to go through! We don't know we're well off, do we, Johnny?"

"That's true. Do you have folks back in Latvia still?"

When Gloria heard that they did, she wanted to know why they didn't come over and join them.

"They wouldn't be allowed out."

"You mean they've got to stay whether they want to or not? Imagine, Johnny, if we couldn't cross the border into the States when we wanted to!"

At the mention of the border, he looked thoughtful. He said to Astra, "How long have you been in Canada?"

"Just a few months."

"You won't be a Canadian citizen, then?"

Astra began to feel uneasy.

"Course she couldn't be, Johnny," said Gloria. "But she's got Canadian papers."

"They'll be landed immigrant papers. You have to be a full Canadian citizen or else have a visa to cross the border. You didn't tell me she wasn't Canadian, Gloria."

"I never thought to. I thought it'd be okay as long as she had Canadian papers."

"Well, you thought wrong."

Astra stared at the rest of her hot dog. She couldn't eat another bite now. After all the excitement, she might

119

not get to see Mara after all. Disappointment was choking her. And any minute now Gloria and Johnny would be having a fight—over her!

"Maybe I could get a bus back," she said miserably.

Gloria was looking at her husband. "Listen, Johnny, nobody bothers about Canadian cars at the border, you know they don't. They just ask where you're born."

"She can't say Latvia!"

"Why couldn't she just say Toronto?"

"Because she doesn't sound as if she comes from Toronto." He pronounced it "Tranha."

"We can't disappoint her. She's set her heart on going, haven't you, Astra? And we can't dump her out here, miles from anywhere, to wait for a bus."

Johnny sighed heavily. "I guess she could say Montreal. That could account for her accent. They'd think she was French Canadian."

"Montreal it is, then! Say Montreal, Astra!"

Astra said it.

"No sweat!" declared Gloria.

Climbing back into the truck, Astra felt queasy in the stomach.

A few miles further on, they saw the border lights and the red rear lights of the cars lining up ahead of them. They slowed. As they approached the barrier, Johnny rolled down his window. Astra thought she was going to be sick, the way she had been at the dog food factory.

The Immigration official leaned over and rested his arm on the windowsill of the car. "Evening, folks. Where you heading?"

"Boston. To see my brother."

"How long are you staying?"

"Monday night."

"Where you born?"

120

"Tranah," said Johnny.

"Tranah," said Gloria.

"How's about you?" The man was peering into the back of the truck now, at Astra. She gulped, took a deep breath, said, "Montreal."

"Okay then, folks, on you go! Have yourselves a good weekend."

"Thanks."

Johnny rolled the window back up. They swept across the border and were in the United States of America.

"Told you it'd be no sweat, didn't I?" said Gloria.

How nice Gloria was turning out to be, thought Astra, as she settled down to try to get some sleep. Yet, in the beginning, she had not taken to her much, had thought her a hard sort of woman. She remembered her mother's advice about not making rash judgments, which brought her thoughts back to Irena. She fell asleep.

The morning light was gray. They emerged, red-eyed and stiff-legged, from the truck into the Boston street. This area of the city was called Back Bay, said Johnny—the name explained itself. You could smell the sea when the wind was in the right direction. Quite a few immigrants lived here.

He had stopped the truck outside the school where Paulis was janitor. Astra hoped that Mara had received her letter. What if the Jansons were away? But no, they wouldn't be. They couldn't be!

As she was getting her bag out of the back of the van, she heard Mara's voice. *"Astra!"*

She dropped the bag and ran to greet her friend. They met with such force that they almost winded each other. They doubled over, gasping for breath, laughing, on the verge of tears.

121

"Oh, Mara, you haven't changed!"

"Did you think I would? It's only been six months."

"But so much has happened."

"You are the same, too."

Johnny brought Astra's bag over to her. "Pick you up Monday afternoon, okay?"

"Okay, Johnny. Thank you, Johnny!"

The Gleggs drove off.

Zigi had come running out of their house, which was next to the school. How was Tomas? Why hadn't he come? Then out ran Klara, and Astra saw a difference in her. "You've grown so, Klara! What a big girl!" And now here were Olga and Paulis.

"*Sveiki!*" Greetings! they called.

Astra hugged them each in turn and passed on messages of greeting from her family.

"Such excitement we have not had for a long time," said Olga, drying her eyes on her apron. "What a big fuss we are making in the street! Come inside, and then you can tell us *all* the news."

"It would take all weekend for that," said Astra, following Olga into her warm kitchen. She always associated Olga with the smell of warm kitchens and of baking. The smell of *pīragī* met her. They were Latvian buns with little pieces of bacon and onions in them. "Oh, Olga, you've remembered how I love them!"

"How would I ever forget that? I've made *pascha*, too, for Easter." *Pascha* was based on the Russian dish made with cottage cheese, butter, eggs, sugar, dried fruit, almonds, lemon peel, and a flavoring of vanilla. The mixture was put into a wooden mold and pressed down with weights to squeeze out the liquid.

"I didn't have a proper mold, so I used a flower pot!"

"It looks wonderful!"

122

"We have three days, Astra," said Mara, smiling. "Almost."

That's not much, Astra thought with a pang, when she considered how she and Mara used to have all the time in the world together. They'd spent lazy summer days wandering through meadows, talking, always talking. But three days would have to do. They would make the most of them.

"You've cut your hair, Mara!" Astra had not noticed in the street.

Mara nodded. "Do you like it?"

"I think so. But I was so used to you with braids."

Mara had had long, thick pigtails that reached to her waist. She said that she was too old for them now. In America girls her age did not have braids.

She was wearing a black ballerina skirt and a white blouse with a little boy collar and a black ribbon! Astra laughed. In her valise she had her blue skirt and white blouse. Together, they would look like two North American girls.

After breakfast Astra went for a walk with Mara, Zigi, and their father. The shops were closed, since it was Good Friday, and the streets were quiet.

"Zigi loves it down here," said Mara. He had run ahead of them. "He likes to watch the ships loading up. He thinks he might go to sea when he leaves school. What about Tomas?"

"He still wants to be an architect."

"Look how many countries the ships are from, Astra!" said Paulis. "They are flying flags from countries all over the world."

"You don't have the sea in Toronto, do you?" asked Mara.

"We have the lake, Lake Ontario. It's so big that it's almost like the sea, and it's got a harbor."

"It can't have a harbor as big as this, though," said Zigi, who had come back to join them.

Hugo and Irena walked along the lakeshore. There were a lot of people out and about, since it was a holiday weekend.

Irena had come to the door of Hugo's room earlier and said, "You're not going to work all day, are you, Hugo, not on Easter Saturday?"

He'd laughed, pushed back his chair from the piece of board he'd rigged up as a desk, and stretched his arms. "It does not sound like a good idea."

"Your head needs a chance to clear itself."

"You could be right, Irena."

"Your mother and father have gone for a walk."

He'd stood up then and said that perhaps they, too, should go for a walk. They had taken the Queen Street streetcar eastward to the area known as the Beaches.

"In summer people sail boats on the lake," said Irena. "I should like to have a boat one day, wouldn't you, Hugo?"

"I would be useless at sailing, I would probably fall overboard! Astra and Tomas would make good sailors. I can imagine them both. They're much better at all these physical things than I am. Especially Tomas."

"I wouldn't be *that* keen to have a boat. Shall we go to a drugstore and have a milk shake? It'll be my treat."

Hugo blushed. He had no money in his pocket, had not thought to bring any.

"That's all right, Hugo. I've got enough." Irena smiled and slipped her hand through the crook of his arm.

* * *

Mara said that she and her friend Janis—she looked at Astra from under lowered eyelids when she said his name—were going to take her to the movies that evening. "It is to be our treat. Then afterwards we shall go to a soda fountain."

Janis came to pick them up after dinner. He had a scrubbed-clean look and wore his hair slicked down with Brylcreem. He was carrying a box of chocolates, which he presented to Mara, who blushed as she accepted them. They looked into each other's eyes like two people with a secret.

At the movie theater, Mara sat in the middle, with Astra on one side and Janis on the other. Mara and Janis held hands, disengaging them only when she wanted to open the candy box to offer another chocolate. Most people around them seemed to be eating popcorn, and making a lot of noise doing it. In the back row couples were spending more time kissing and giggling than watching the movie. The audience was made up mostly of couples, Astra observed. She was definitely the odd one out.

The first film was a Western, full of cowboys thundering over plains and whirling lassos. The music was loud and fast-paced, in keeping with the thud of horses' hooves and the crackle of gunshots. There were many hectic gunfights and much chasing of the bad men by the good men through low, scrub-covered hills. Astra had not been to the movies since they'd arrived in Canada, but it seemed that Mara and Janis went regularly. Mara kept whispering to her, telling her that this was the second feature, and then there'd be an intermission, and after that the main feature. This was the reverse of how their relationship used to be. She, Astra, had always been the one to lead, to know more about everything than Mara. For the first few minutes she resented it, then she gave herself a good talking to! She was glad Mara was settling in so well and had found a nice young man. And if she were to come and visit them in Toronto, then it would be Astra who would take control of the situation. This was Mara's territory.

Afterward, as promised, they went to a soda fountain. It was crowded with young couples, many of whom might have been at the movies. They found seats in a side booth, and Janis went up to the counter. The room was noisy, with the chatter of voices and music spilling from a machine called a jukebox. Blue fumes of cigarette smoke spiraled up toward the ceiling.

On his way back to join them, Janis put coins in the jukebox. Out came the song, "You'd Be So Nice To Come Home To." Janis set three glasses of Coke on the table, and he and Mara looked into each other's eyes again and smiled. Astra thought that, if she were to slip away, they would not notice.

"Coke, Astra?" said Mara. Her smile was blinding.

They sat in the booth, drank Coke, and talked about the town of Cesis in Latvia and their memories of it. It seemed a long, long way from Boston.

On Easter Sunday morning, Hugo, Tomas, and their parents went to a Latvian church service. The first Latvian church in Toronto had been founded only on March 13. Until they could afford a building of their own, they were being allowed to hold services in the German Lutheran church on Bond Street.

The Latvian pastor welcomed the congregation. For many—most—it was their first Easter in Toronto. Latvian silver and amber jewelry was much in evidence. Scarcely a word of English was to be heard.

126

"It could be Riga—or Cesis!" Kristina smiled.

Afterward, the Petersons mingled with the congregation and found several old friends and acquaintances. Some had been in the camp in Esslingen. Others had known them from Riga days, when Lukas had been a professor at the university. News was exchanged, also addresses. Promises to visit were made.

"It will be nice to have some visitors," said Lukas. "It will be more like the old days." The door of their house had always been open, and it was seldom that they had sat down to a meal without a guest or two. To feed extra people now would be more of a problem, but no one would mind what they were given. To come and talk and renew old friendships was the important thing.

Alighting from the streetcar on the way back, they met Mrs. Simmonds and Irena, returning from their church. Both wore dashing Easter bonnets, trimmed with ribbons and decked with taffeta roses. Irena had made the hats. Kristina complimented her. Irena smiled, pleased. She said she enjoyed making things. Her mother said that she was very creative.

They walked home together, the young ones going out in front, the parents coming behind. All were agreed that Easter was a happy time of year. It was good to know that the long, dark winter was behind them and ahead lay warmth and lengthening days.

When they reached the house, Mrs. Simmonds invited the Petersons to join her and Irena for lunch. She had put a large chicken in the oven, and Irena had made an Easter cake.

"We will never be able to eat it all ourselves."

The Simmonds' invitation was warmly accepted by the Petersons.

* * *

127

"Now you must show Astra everything!" commanded Olga, as they rose from lunch. She would not allow anyone to help with the cleaning up. "No, away you go, you young people, and enjoy the sunshine!" She escorted them to the door, giving Mara instructions.

"Take her to Copley Square. And to the Common. And the Public Gardens. And don't forget Beacon Hill! Boston is a fine city, Astra. You will be able to tell Kristina and Lukas all about it."

"Listen to her!" Paulis stood beside his wife in the doorway, with his arms around her waist, smiling. "You would think she had been here for years! She has only been downtown twice."

Olga good-naturedly dug him in the stomach with her elbow. "I am too busy to go downtown, I am working hard all day long!"

Astra, Mara, and Janis walked in the gardens and on the Common. Mara and Janis walked arm in arm. They ate ice cream, which Astra insisted on paying for.

"You can't pay for everything, Janis!" She knew he would not have much money, that he would be trying to save, like every other DP who wanted to make his way and lead a better life. Their night out at the movies and soda fountain had probably used up his month's spending allowance. He lived with his family in a tiny tenement apartment in an area that Mara said was not much more than a slum.

"It's very crowded, with many people in each apartment. Several families have to share the same lavatory, the way we often had to do in the camps. There are rats, too. We were very lucky to get our house with Father's job." It was a stout two-story stone house, with three bedrooms, a kitchen, and a bathroom. Olga was proud of it, kept it shining like a newly minted dollar piece.

Astra was not invited to Janis's home. Instead, Olga

asked his family to their house on Sunday evening. They spent a good evening eating, drinking, and recalling Latvian days. Janis's father, who was a plumber, had done work for Astra's grandmother in her house in Cesis!

"I put in a new bathroom for her before the war. How is she now, your grandmother?"

"Not good, we think. But we hear very little."

"Ah well, one day we shall all go home," said Janis's mother.

Shall we? wondered Astra. Janis's family talked as if the Soviet Union might collapse at any time. They said that President Truman would make Moscow give the Baltic states back to their own people.

"They say he is a good man, President Truman. He will see to it that justice is done."

Astra did not argue, did not point out that the Cold War—which was what the strained relationship between East and West had come to be called—seemed to be growing chillier daily, with each side becoming more and more suspicious of the other. Some said the Cold War might become World War III—a prospect that made her shiver. She wondered how Janis's mother could think that justice would be done. Their own experiences had surely taught them not to expect it! But it was not an evening for political talk, which would only lead to gloom.

When they were getting ready for bed, she said to Mara, trying to speak lightly, "I don't seem to have seen much of you on your own!"

"I know! We can talk now, though. But you do like Janis, don't you?" Mara was anxious.

"Of course. He's a very nice boy."

"It would be terrible for me if you and Janis were not to like each other—my two best friends in the world!"

* * *

Their parting was painful, and they both had to fight back tears. Mara promised that she would come to Toronto next. She would find a way somehow or other. They knew, however, that promises were easier to make than to keep. And Mara's life, from now on, would be turning more and more toward Janis.

Olga gave Astra a bag of *pīragī* for her mother. They were still warm from the oven.

"Give them all our love, and tell them to come visit us in Boston, too!"

Astra waved until they turned the corner and the Jansons were out of sight.

"Nice folks," commented Gloria. "You can come back with us to see them next Easter."

"She'll need to get a visa first," said Johnny, reminding Astra that there was a border to cross going back.

What if they didn't let her in? But she wouldn't be entitled to stay in the States, either.

"Don't worry," said Gloria, settling down to light a cigarette. "Just do the same as you did before."

Astra was on edge, nevertheless, all the way to the border. This was worse, in a way, than coming in. Then she could only have been turned back. Now she could be arrested for having entered the United States illegally.

"Stop worrying, I tell you!" said Gloria.

It was all right for Gloria—*she* was a Canadian citizen. She had rights. She belonged.

It was dark by the time they reached the border, and Astra was glad of that. Traffic was busy with Easter vacationers going home.

"Make out you're sleeping," said Gloria.

Astra covered herself with a blanket and put her head down.

They were waved through U.S. Immigration and

stopped by the Canadian official. He asked to see the car documents. He held them under the light to study them, did not just give them a casual glance. He did not look as friendly as the official had on their outward journey.

Then he began to question them. Where had they been? For what purpose, and so forth.

"And where were you born?"

The Gleggs in unison said Toronto.

"And your friend in the back?"

"Montreal," said Gloria loudly and clearly. Too loudly, thought Astra, whose heart was thudding so hard she wondered the man did not hear it.

"Montreal eh?" He looked over Johnny's shoulder.

Astra lifted her head to meet his eyes. They seemed small and narrowed in the dim light. He was waiting for her to speak. She swallowed, said "Montreal."

"Et puis, vous parlez français, mademoiselle?"

Oh no, a French-speaking customs official! Or perhaps they all were, but some didn't bother to show off their French.

"Oui," she said weakly. She knew no more than two dozen words in French. *Je suis malade.* She felt ill. Could she say that?

The man seemed to hesitate for a moment, then he waved his hand. *"Allez-en!"*

"That was a close shave!" said Gloria, as Johnny accelerated and swept them over the border.

They were back in Canada. Back home. "Yes, home!" Astra repeated to herself. She had not thought of it in that way before. But coming back—returning—that was the word that leaped to mind.

Able to relax now, she could settle down to think about the weekend. Last night, in bed, she and Mara had talked for hours, as they used to do, and Mara had

131

confided that she and Janis hoped to marry one day, but not yet, not for a long time. They would have to work hard and save money first.

"I am so pleased that I will marry a Latvian, Astra. It's much better to marry one of your own kind, don't you think?"

Astra had shrugged. She had not given much thought to marrying.

Mara was looking for another job, one that would enable her to earn more money. Everyone talked constantly about working hard and earning money. Well, it was what they had to do. When you started with nothing, you had no other option.

Before Astra drifted off into a doze, she had made a resolution: She was going to start doing some of the things girls her age in North America did. She was going to have her hair cut in the pageboy style, turned under at the ends, and with bangs across the forehead. It was very fashionable, Nancy had told her, and it would suit her. And she was going to let Nancy take her dancing at the Palace Pier.

TEN

THE PALACE PIER was right on the lakeshore. The streetcar was packed with men in dark suits and slicked-down hair, girls in swirling skirts and mouths bright with lipstick. Astra followed Nancy down the stairs, watching as her own blue ballerina skirt billowed out around her. With her pay that week she had bought a new pair of black suede pumps. Nancy was wearing high, white, ankle-strap shoes, a petunia pink skirt, a wide black cummerbund, and a white crepe rayon blouse, all tucks and ruffles. She had bought the blouse on the way home from work that afternoon, at Eaton's. It had cost five dollars and fifty cents.

"Worth it, though," she said, shifting a wad of chewing gum into her cheek.

Earrings swayed from her ears, bangles spun on her wrists.

"You've got to make the guys notice you," she said.

The crowd streamed toward the dance hall, Nancy and Astra moving in its wake. Astra felt a queasiness in her stomach. The only dances she had ever been to had

133

been those at school in Esslingen. There she had been surrounded by friends of both sexes, had known virtually everyone. They'd been informal affairs, and no one had been particularly dressed up. It hadn't mattered. They had always enjoyed themselves.

They bought their tickets, and Nancy led the way into the ladies' room. The air was heavy with the smell of face powder and perfume. In front of the long mirror girls were lined up, reapplying lipstick on mouths already well colored, combing and rearranging their hair, checking the seams of their stockings. Astra hung back.

"Come on!" urged Nancy, pushing through to make a space for them.

Astra gazed at herself in the mirror. With her skirt she wore her white blouse and her string of amber beads. They were one of the few things about her that looked familiar. She touched the side of her head. She was still trying to get used to the sight of herself with her new haircut. Nancy said it made her look more modern and more glamorous. Nancy scoured glossy women's magazines for tips on "How To Make Yourself More Glamorous." She was singing "Dance, Ballerina, Dance!" to herself and swaying her hips as if she were already on the dance floor. Astra wished she could go home.

"Next week I'm gonna buy myself an eight-gored black taffeta skirt," said Nancy, as she tightened her cummerbund to make her waist look smaller. "Thirteen bucks ninety-five cents."

"That's more than half your pay."

"Who cares."

She gave her mother seven dollars a week for board and kept the rest.

"Okay, kid!" she said, and led the way into the dance hall.

134

The floor was large, a bit like an arena, with small tables set around it, and a stage at one end, on which the band played. A singer was crooning into the microphone in the style of the film star Bing Crosby. "I'll Be Seeing You in All the Old Familiar Places." Astra longed to see a familiar face among all these unknown ones. She thought of Markus, her Esslingen boyfriend, now living in Edinburgh, Scotland, on the other side of the Atlantic ocean. If only he could be here. What fun they would have! But harping on the past would get her nowhere. She remembered her resolution on the journey back from Boston and sat down beside Nancy.

"Smile, kid, smile! Look as if you're having a good time! You'd think you were pressing trouser bottoms on a hot day! And if any guy wants to take you for a drink, that's fine with me. It's everyone for herself, okay?"

Astra nodded.

A man was approaching their table. Nancy began to talk even more animatedly, turning toward Astra, not looking in his direction.

"Wasn't that a hoot today when that guy came in and asked if he could keep his trousers on while they were being cleaned!" She exploded into laughter, and her earrings swung to and fro, her bangles jangled, and the table shook.

The man stretched out his arm and tapped her on the shoulder. She glanced up in apparent surprise.

"Care to dance?"

"Why, sure." She flashed him a wide smile. "Excuse me, Astra."

Astra watched the man lead Nancy onto the floor, put his arm around her waist, and swing her into the midst of the other dancers. Whenever they came around and passed her table, Nancy broke off her chatter to give

Astra a little wave. She appeared to be talking nonstop, as well as smiling.

When the final chords of the number crashed out, accompanied by a roll on the drums, the man escorted Nancy back to her seat.

"Thanks." She bestowed on him another smile. "That was great."

He returned to stand among the other men who were lined up along the edge of the dance floor. Astra was conscious of their eyes roving the room, jumping over each of the girls in turn, assessing them. Nancy took her powder compact from her bag and, peering into the small mirror, dabbed at her cheeks with the pink puff.

"I use green powder for dances."

"Green?"

"It stops you looking too flushed."

"You seemed to like him."

"Who?"

"Your partner."

"Him? He was a drag."

The Master of Ceremonies was stepping up to the microphone. He, too, was smiling. What a lot of smiling went on! And flashing of white teeth. Astra wondered that their cheeks didn't ache from the effort. The M.C. cleared his throat. "This is your big chance, ladies!" he announced, and paused so that the ladies could cheer.

"Ladies' choice!" cried Nancy. "Come on, Astra! Let's go pick a couple of guys!"

Astra shook her head as Nancy tried to pull her up. "No, please, I'd rather not."

"Don't be such a dumbbell!" Most of the other girls were on their feet. "Okay, suit yourself. I'm not going to miss out." And Nancy was off skating across the floor, her petunia pink skirt flying.

136

Astra saw her walk up and down the line of men, looking them over. Then she pounced. Her choice was a tall, dark-haired man about ten years older than herself. His smile matched hers.

Astra retreated to the ladies' room, which was empty. She stared at herself in the mirror, wrinkling her nose. She didn't think she would ever have what it took to make a man at the Palace Pier ballroom ask her to dance. And she wasn't sure that she even wanted to have it.

She hung around in the powder room until she reckoned the ladies' choice would be over. Nancy gave her a talking to when she came back.

"Do you want to have a good time or don't you?"

"I don't know."

"If you sit here all night like a dummy, nobody'll ever ask you to dance. Guys like to feel you're in demand."

"I can't help it if I'm not."

"Sure you can. You know what your trouble is, Astra? You're too serious. Loosen up, relax! Let go, baby! Let go!" Nancy snapped her fingers and rocked on her chair.

The music started up again. The dark-haired man with the smile came back to reclaim Nancy. She appeared to melt into his arms, and before the dance was halfway through they were dancing cheek to cheek. And when it was over, he took her off to another table.

Astra opened her bag and looked inside, even though she knew there was nothing in there to occupy her. She wished she'd brought a book, but it would hardly do to be seen reading at the Palace Pier. She closed the bag again, looked around. Everyone seemed to be with somebody, either in couples, male and female, or two girls together, and in some cases three or four. Well, so what! She shouldn't care about being conspicuous. But

137

she did care, though. Then she thought that she probably wasn't conspicuous at all; no one was taking any notice of her.

When she was about to get up and go, she felt a touch on her arm. She looked around.

A boy about her own age, perhaps a year or two older, was standing there.

"Would you like to dance?"

She hesitated. She almost said "Thanks, but I'm just leaving," and then she took another look at him. He had friendly brown eyes and a slightly humorous quirk to his mouth. And he was not flashing dazzling white teeth.

"Okay, thank you." She got up and took the hand he was holding out.

The dance was a slow waltz. She had learned to waltz when she was quite young in Latvia. And Nancy had clued her in on the kinds of things to talk and not to talk about while dancing. "Don't start going on about German literature or any of that stuff! He might think you're an egghead. Nothing turns a guy off more than that."

Astra allowed her partner to open up the conversation.

"Do you come here often?" he asked after they'd done a few turns and she had realized that she could dance better than he could. He kept stepping on the toes of her new suede pumps. "Don't say it's your first time," Nancy had told her. "He'll think you're a greenhorn. Act like you know your way around."

"No," said Astra, "not often." Then she added, "This is the first time."

He laughed. "Me too!"

Now she laughed, for the first time that evening. Nancy, revolving past in the arms of her partner, raised her thumb with approval.

Hugo lifted his head from his trigonometry book and looked out of the window. It was a mild evening in early May, and not yet quite dark. He stretched his arms out wide. He felt restless. He was fed up with working!

Tomas was at a friend's, and Astra had gone dancing at the Palace Pier. She had wanted him to go with her and her friend Nancy. He'd said she must be joking! He couldn't imagine himself there, and Nancy, whom he'd met when he'd called for Astra at the shop, terrified him with her fast talk and the way she flapped her thickly mascarad eyelashes. He hadn't known what to say to her.

The only dancing he'd done had been in Germany, with Bettina, at the local inn on a Sunday evening. You couldn't call that a dance hall, no matter how far you stretched your imagination. An accordionist had squeezed out the tunes for them to dance to. Bettina had taught him to do the waltz in the Schneiders' kitchen. She'd been patient; she'd had to be. Nancy did not seem at all patient. She had talked about big bands, quick-steps, and fox-trots. She couldn't get over his not knowing about musicians like Harry James and Les Brown. "You're kidding!" she'd said.

He turned, hearing a soft tap on the door, and said, "Come in."

The door opened a crack.

"Are you busy?" asked Irena. "Could you help me with my math? I just can't make out this problem at all."

"Of course."

She brought the book to him, and they pored over it. He saw her difficulty right away.

"You're brilliant at math."

"You're brilliant at being a librarian."

They laughed.

She leaned across his desk to look at the picture of Bettina on his shelf.

"She's very pretty. It must be difficult being engaged to someone so far away?"

He nodded. "Though I'm so busy—"

"You don't have much time to think about it, I guess?"

"It's not that." He shrugged. "It's just that there's no choice at the moment."

"You were young to get engaged, Mother says."

"Perhaps." He did not want to talk about it. It had all come about naturally enough at the time. They'd been in love—*were* in love. *Was* he in love with Bettina now? He could not cope with that question, did not know the answer to it. Sometimes he felt he could scarcely remember her; so much separated them. Time, distance, experience. And then, at other times, the image of her face would come to him so sharply, and he would remember the sound of her laugh so clearly, that he would feel a terrible ache inside.

He looked at Irena. She was wearing a deep blue blouse that matched her eyes. And she had unbraided her pale blonde hair and brushed it out so that it hung loosely over her shoulders. She was an attractive girl, and he liked her. And he was aware that she liked him. She did not try to hide it. It made him feel good to know that she liked him. And why should she not? They were two people who enjoyed each other's company, who liked to read books and to listen to music, and who had many things to talk about. They had much in common. They were friends. So what would be the harm in going for a stroll together through the soft May evening and

140

stopping at a soda fountain for a milk shake? It was what most boys his age would be doing on such an evening.

"Would you like to go out, Irena? Now, I mean. With me."

Her face lit up. "Oh, I would, Hugo."

While she went to fetch her jacket, Hugo looked in on his parents, who were entertaining a couple from Riga. They had begun exchanging visits with other Latvians whom they had met at church. He could hear the chatter of their voices as he went down the stairs.

He shook hands with the visitors and told his parents he was going out for a while. As he closed the door, he thought how much better his mother and father were looking. Kristina, although still out every day at her cleaning job, seemed less tired. She said she would go on working as long as they needed the money. Every little bit helped. They were putting a few dollars away each week in a savings fund. Their home fund, they called it. Lukas said it would help them either to buy a house here or, if a miracle occurred, to return to Latvia. They must still hope for that return. He had found some work too, translating, and was pleased about that, even though it paid little. He had hated being the only one in the family not working.

Hugo ducked his head to look in the hall mirror and smooth down his hair. He wondered if he should try to flatten it with Brylcreem, but Astra had said not to dare! She hated boys with greasy heads. He straightened his new glasses, which he'd saved for and bought only the week before. They'd replaced the wire ones made for him in Hamburg just before the Allies came in to occupy it. Another bit of his past gone—though he had not been able to bring himself to throw them in the garbage. They

141

had meant so much to him at the time; they'd restored sight to him after months of being semi-blind. They had been bought for him by Bettina's father.

Irena was waiting for him on the porch. The air smelled of spring, of fresh earth and blossoms waiting to burst out. A robin was chirping on the topmost branch of the lilac tree, his rounded breast silhouetted against the darkening blue of the sky.

As Hugo stepped out into the street with Irena, it seemed only natural to turn and take her hand.

Tomas was at his friend Don's house, in the garage, negotiating to buy a bicycle. Don had been given a new one for his birthday, with whitewall balloon tires and chrome mudguards, and he was willing to sell his old one.

"Gee, I don't know how much to ask." Don scratched the back of his head. "How much've you got?"

Tomas held out his dollars. "Seven." He'd gotten three of them by collecting empty bottles in parks and along the lakeshore and claiming the two cents deposit. Hugo and Astra had each given him another dollar, and he'd taken two from his own pay.

"Okay, that sounds fine to me."

The money and the bicycle changed hands. Tomas was pleased enough with his purchase. The bike was not in great shape, was pretty scuffed, and the brakes didn't work very well, but he could fix all that. He planned to repaint the frame in two tones of blue, had already picked out the shades. He'd picked out new dark blue mudguards, too, and would get those as soon as he'd saved up again.

At last he had a bike of his own! Now he could go for rides with Don and Sandy on Sundays. He wasn't allowed to bring the grocery bike home, not that he would have wanted to. It was too old-fashioned. He wouldn't be seen dead riding that stuffy-looking thing except when he was working.

He was pretty fed up with working. Having to go there every single afternoon after school and all day Saturday was getting to him. He'd be working while his friends were playing basketball or tennis or going swimming. He'd tried looking for something else, but the only other job he could have gotten was delivering morning papers, and that paid peanuts. There was nothing he could do except go on with Mr. Zawacki. He wanted a bike like Don's, and the only way he'd be able to get it would be to work for it.

"Want a game of Ping-Pong?" asked Don.

They went down to the rec room in the basement. Don's mother called out to them. Did they want a soda pop? She brought them one each and a plate of cookies. She stayed a moment to talk.

"How're things with you then, Tom?"

"Pretty good." Except for Mr. Zawacki, Tomas went on to tell her; he was getting on his nerves. "Whatever I do is wrong. He's so fussy. If I drop a grain of sugar, he hits the roof. 'How can I make profit when you throw my goods on floor?' " Tomas mimicked Mr. Zawacki's accent.

"He's excitable, I guess. You know, Tom, your English is coming along well. I notice a difference, I really do. You talk almost like a Canadian boy now—no, I really mean it."

Tomas was pleased with the compliment. He knew he didn't talk *quite* like a Canadian boy, but he was getting there. It was only occasionally now that he made a blooper in class and sent everyone into convulsions of laughter.

The boys played Ping-Pong for an hour, and then Tomas set off to ride his bike home. Fortunately, the lights were working.

He took a longer route back so that he would have more time to try out the machine. He rode slowly, knowing the brakes wouldn't hold if he had to stop in a hurry. He tried out the bell. It sounded a bit flat. A new one shouldn't cost too much. And a bit of oil in the brakes would help them—a boy in his class had given him the tip. He couldn't wait to start stripping down the frame and repainting it.

A couple of streets along he passed Carol—she of the long pigtails and the bows who sat in front of him at school—walking with her mother. But her braids had been lopped off! Her hair had been cut into a bob. He didn't recognize her until she turned her head.

"Hi, Tom!" she said, in a grown-up sort of way, and as if they were the best of friends.

"Oh—hi there, Carol!" He swerved, straightened, and stood up on the pedals to put on a burst of speed, aware that she would be watching him.

On the next corner he passed Hugo and Irena. They were walking hand in hand. They didn't notice him until he'd rung his bell three times.

They looked around and waved, using their free hands, not dropping their joined ones. And then they continued along the road, not even interested enough to stop and look at his new bike.

"Who's taking you home tonight?" the soloist asked, clutching the microphone close to his chest. It was the last dance, and Astra was dancing it with Drew. He'd introduced himself to her after their first dance. "I'm Drew Johnstone." "Astra Petersons." They'd shaken hands. He'd already learned she was from Latvia. Well, of course he'd been immediately aware that she had an accent, though he'd complimented her on her English. He'd bought her a Coke, and they'd stayed together for the rest of the evening, occasionally dancing, more often just sitting at a table talking. He was a first-year medical student at the University of Toronto, had been born and brought up in the city.

The singer finished his song, the drums rolled, the dancers clapped.

Drew asked, "Can I take you home?"

"Be careful," Nancy had warned Astra. "If someone asks to take you home, make sure he doesn't try to get too fresh with you—*especially* if he's got a car. On the streetcar he can't get into much trouble."

"I've got a car."

"A car?"

"It's a bit of a wreck but it goes. Don't worry—you won't have to push it!"

"Oh, I wasn't worrying—"

"Good! Shall we go, then?" He put his hand under her elbow. He left her outside the ladies' and said he'd see her at the door.

Nancy came rushing in behind her, wanting to know what he was like, what he did, what his father did, where he lived, had he asked to take her home?

"He's got a car."

"Watch it then, kiddo!"

"I think I can take care of myself." Astra grinned. "I'm no weakling."

"I wonder if he'll ask you for a date. Sometimes they ask for your phone number, and you never hear from them again. U of T medicine, eh? Not bad. Doctors earn a pile. There could be a future in it, gal."

"I hardly think I'm going to marry him! I've just met him."

They walked out together. Nancy's partner was waiting for her. They said their goodnights, and Drew took Astra's hand and led her away.

A slight drizzle of rain was falling, shrouding the lake and blurring the city lights. Astra was glad that she had not worn her raincoat; when it got damp, it still gave off the odor of skunk. Even dry cleaning had not removed it completely. Kristina said she was imagining things. But on wet days Astra hated to go on the streetcar, in case people would notice her and turn away.

Drew's car, a Ford convertible and not looking that much of a wreck, was parked farther along the road. He opened the passenger door for her and helped her in. He had good manners. She liked that. Some boys were very casual and had no manners at all, would walk through a door in front of you, so Nancy said. Everything Astra knew about Canadian boys came from Nancy. Nancy could talk about boys for hours. Astra had learned nothing in that line from Irena. It was seldom that she and Irena exchanged more than a few basic words.

"Okay?" asked Drew.

"Fine, thank you."

They didn't say much else. Astra felt suddenly shy now that she was alone with this stranger, sealed off from the world. In the dance hall there had been music and other people around them. They sped through the streets of late-night Toronto. She stared straight ahead. He knew the street where she lived, since it was close to the university. Quite a lot of students roomed around there, he said. He lived at home with his parents.

He pulled up in front of the Simmonds' door. The windows were dark. She had never been out so late in the city.

"Can I call you?"

"All right." She gave him the phone number, and he

146

wrote it down in a notebook that seemed to be crammed with phone numbers. Were they from other girls? Perhaps they were. He must know lots of girls in Toronto. He had lived here all his life, after all, and was not like her, who knew very few people. Perhaps, as Nancy said, she would never see him again, and he was asking for her number merely out of politeness and to make it easier to say good night.

She opened her door. He got out and joined her on the pavement. They stood a little awkwardly.

"Thank you for bringing me home."

"A pleasure. I've enjoyed the evening."

"So have I."

He leaned over and kissed her on the cheek. Then he turned and went back around to the driver's side of the car.

She let herself into the house. She took off her shoes and tiptoed up the stairs, humming softly to herself the tune of "Dance, Ballerina, Dance!"

ELEVEN

"I T'S ALWAYS BETTER when they ask you for a date right
away," said Nancy. She and Astra were sitting in
the back room. They were eating their lunch and
having a postmortem on Saturday night. "But the next
best thing is if he asks for your phone number."

Her partner had asked for hers but had not gotten it.
He'd turned out to be a bit "on the fresh side." Astra
wasn't surprised to hear that and wondered why Nancy,
with all her knowledge in this field, hadn't seen it too.
"I just told him I wasn't that kind of gal." Nancy took
another bite of her peanut butter and jelly sandwich.
"Plenty more fish in the sea. That's what you've always
got to remember, Astra! Don't let him think he matters
too much."

A whole day had elapsed since Saturday night. Drew
could have phoned yesterday. But Nancy said that they
didn't often phone on Sunday after meeting you on Saturday night—they mightn't want to seem too eager, they
might be busy with family. She thought he looked as if he
came from one of Toronto's "top drawer" families that

lived in places like Forest Hill or Rosedale. "He had that look about him. Kind of as if he's not had to grub for anything. I guess his father's probably a doctor or a lawyer."

"A lawyer."

"See—what did I tell you? You can always spot them. They're usually English or Scots descent. They run the city." Nancy's own father was of Ukrainian stock, her mother Polish. She tore open a bag of potato chips. "He'd be a good catch."

"I don't want to catch him."

"Don't you?" asked Nancy skeptically.

Thinking about Drew helped Astra get through the afternoon. The weather had turned warmer, and it was stuffy in the workroom. By the end of the day the steam rising up from the trouser press was becoming trying. Sometimes she thought that if she had to pres one more pair of trousers, she would scream. She had various ways of coping with the tedium, reciting poetry to herself, conjugating German verbs, talking to Mara in her head. Today, her diversion was her Saturday night partner.

She hurried home after work. She knew it was unlikely he would have phoned during the day, but she paused in the hall to glance at the notepad beside the phone. Nothing there. Hugo and Tomas came in, and they ate, and during the meal Astra kept her ear cocked. The phone rang, and she felt her face turn warm. She heard Irena going into the hall to answer it. "Oh, hi there, Angie!" Astra picked up her knife and fork again. It was one of their class nights; they would be out for two to three hours.

She let Hugo go ahead of her. She said to her mother, "Someone may phone. Could you listen for it?"

Kristina looked surprised. It was not often that any of them received a phone call.

"Nancy said she might call," said Astra and hurried out, wondering why she had lied to her mother. Was she afraid that Drew might *not* call?

She had to concentrate in the German class; the exams were coming too close to waste any time. Occasionally though, her thoughts strayed, and she wondered what Drew would be doing. How could she have any idea about his life?

After the class she sometimes went for a coffee or a Coke with Hugo and Irena. It had become an awkward threesome, with Hugo in the middle, having to be the pivot on which any conversation could turn. So far Astra had stubbornly refused to give up going, not prepared to be ousted by Irena. They were just good friends, Hugo and Irena, so *he* said, and if that was the case, Astra thought, then there was no reason why she shouldn't join them.

But tonight she said, "I think I'll just go on home. I've got an essay I want to start."

She saw the look of relief on Irena's face.

When she got in, Kristina said, "Nancy didn't phone, dear."

"I wish Astra liked me more." Irena twirled the straw around in her Coke and sighed.

"I'm sure she does like you," Hugo mumbled. Why did girls insist on chewing over all this stuff!

"No, I don't believe she does, not much." Irena looked pensive. "You don't think she could be jealous of me, do you?"

Hugo raised one shoulder in a shrug.

"Because we're getting close? I guess we are kind of close?" she asked softly, lifting her deep blue eyes to engage his.

"I suppose."

"We are, *aren't* we, Hugo?"

He gazed back at her miserably. What she said was true, and yet there was Bettina, to whom he was betrothed, and of whom he was deeply fond. But she was not here. It was a shameful thought to have. Out of sight, out of mind? And yet some said absence made the heart grow fonder. You could look at it whatever way you wanted to, depending on your mood. The trouble was that his own mood varied.

Irena put out her hand and rested it over his where it lay on the table. Her touch sent a little tremor up his spine.

"You do like me, don't you, Hugo?"

He nodded. "Yes, I do, Irena. Very much."

Astra wrote a letter to Mara. It was another way of having a conversation with herself. "I met this boy on Saturday night. He's Canadian, and he seemed to like me, but I don't know how to judge whether he really did or not. I know it's silly to be bothered because he hasn't phoned yet—it's only two days. But you know me, Mara—I'm the impatient kind who can't stand waiting! I like to know about things, one way or the other. And, stupid idiot that I am, I thought he would probably ring the very next day. He said he'd enjoyed the evening, and I was sure he meant it. But enjoying an evening might not mean wanting to see you again.

"Maybe you're right—it might be better to go out with Latvian boys! But I don't know any here, not the right age. And Hugo's friend at work, Kostas, who's Lithuanian, is far too old for me."

She got up to lean out of the window. Hugo and Irena hadn't come back yet. Then she saw them turning the corner. They had their arms around each other's waists. So they'd moved on from holding hands!

151

Astra went back to her letter. "I'm fed up with this boy business and worrying if someone likes you! I'm going to move on, pass my exams, and work hard for the next couple of years so that I can get into the university. Then I'll get a good job and make my fortune!"

The next day Nancy and Astra went to the movies after work. They had a hamburger first. The weather had turned warmer, and Nancy was wearing a flowered cotton dress and white, strapped shoes. She seemed to spend most of her pay on clothes.

She eyed the heavy navy blue serge skirt that Astra wore most days to work. "You should get rid of that. It doesn't do a thing for you."

As they walked along to the movie house, Nancy sang, "You're Nobody Till Somebody Loves You."

"You don't believe that, do you, Nancy?"

"Sure I do. Every girl needs a guy."

They joined the line outside the theater. Nancy leaned against the wall and took up a new song, "People Will Say We're in Love." She sighed. "I wish I was in love. But what do I meet all the time—screwballs!"

Glancing up the street at the strolling evening crowd, Astra suddenly spotted Drew. He was with a girl who had long, bouncy blonde hair and who was wearing a full pink cotton skirt and pink lipstick that was a perfect match—who looked as if she came from a similar "top drawer" background. They were walking hand in hand. The girl was chattering, tipping back her head to look up at his face. They were coming past the people on line. Astra's hands moved down to try to cover her skirt, conscious of what a frump she must look.

Drew's face flushed at the moment of recognition, as did hers, though she realized that there was no real reason why either of them should be embarrassed. They had danced for an evening together, and he had taken her home. But he had made no promises, nor were they under any obligation to each other. Neither spoke. He and the girl passed by.

"What a creep!" Nancy had pushed herself off the wall and was standing with her hands parked on her hips, watching them go. "I tell you, Astra, you can't trust any man. Talk about double-crossing, low down—"

"I expect she's a student," said Astra. How she longed to be a student, lead a student's life, and not have to work in a hot, steamy dry cleaner's.

"I don't care what *she* is! It's *him*—"

"Forget it, Nancy." People were turning to look at them. Astra tugged at Nancy's arm. She wanted to forget the incident. Nothing had happened anyway. It was a non-incident. But in spite of all her rationalizing, her pride was wounded and she couldn't help feeling rejected.

"He's not worth bothering about, Astra. He's full of himself, you could see that. Just you wait—you'll meet someone better this Saturday at the Pier."

But there was one thing Astra did know for sure, and that was that she could not face another Saturday night at the Palace Pier, at least not yet.

Kostas was smiling when he arrived at work.

"Come for lunch with me, Hugo. In a café. I will treat you. There is something I have to tell you."

Hugo hesitated, thinking of Irena, who would be expecting him at the library.

"Forget your library and your books for one day!"

"Oh, okay. But just let me stop in on the way."

Kostas waited outside, while Hugo went in.

Irena was not pleased. "But I have been looking forward to seeing you, Hugo! I've been waiting all morning."

"It's just this once, Irena. Kostas is my friend, and he has some special news."

"Why can't he tell you at work? You see him all day long."

"Shush!" said a woman, giving them an angry look.

"I'm sorry, Irena, but I'll have to go." Hugo edged away from the counter. "Kostas is waiting, and we don't get much time off. I'll see you later."

"Maybe!"

Kostas took Hugo to a hamburger place, and they had a double cheeseburger each with french fries and coleslaw.

"You will never guess, Hugo—I have bought a plot of land!"

"Land?"

"Yes, land. For seven hundred dollars. It's *mine*. I'm going to build a house on it. I've saved a thousand dollars, so I've got some left to get going on."

As well as working on the construction site, Kostas had a job as caretaker of a small block of offices. His duties were minimal, but he was expected to be there at night, and in return he got a free apartment, with free heat and light. It meant that he had to spend money only on food and clothing.

"I reckon I can build a house myself. Lots of people are doing it. All sorts of DPs are. And we have experience, don't we, from our work?" Kostas could not stop smiling. "On Sunday I shall take you to see it."

Throughout the afternoon Hugo thought of Kostas' plot of land and seven hundred dollars. It was not *so* much money. They had almost that in the bank, counting the Frasers' five hundred, which they intended to return at some point in the future, but only when they were properly on their feet. Ivar Fraser had written to say they were not even to think of repaying it.

154

On Sunday Astra went with them to look over the plot of land. They took the Yonge Street streetcar out to the city limits, then a bus north to Willowdale. They passed through farmland. Cows were grazing in the fields.

Alighting from the bus, they found themselves in the middle of a subdevelopment. The land had been divided into plots, and houses of varying shapes and sizes were in the process of being built. The roads were muddy and unpaved, but Kostas said that essential services like sanitation and water supplies had already been laid in.

His plot was narrow, but as he pointed out, most of the houses in Toronto were built on narrow strips, with not much space between them. But a decent-sized house could be built on the plot, and there'd still be a piece left over at the back for a garden. Plots around here were costing between six hundred and a thousand.

"First of all, I must build the basement—it is essential because of the frost. I'll make it four or five feet below ground, and three above. Then I'll put floor joists on top and cover it with tar paper, to keep out the rain. Then I shall live in the basement until I can afford to build the next story."

"What a good idea," said Astra.

"Come and I'll show you."

Kostas took them farther along the road to where someone had done just what he proposed. The construction looked squat and odd, with its flat, black tar-paper roof and only three feet of wall visible. Small windows were set in the walls. A light could be seen. A family was living inside, said Kostas. They were from Croatia—another country that had disappeared off the map.

"It *is* an idea, isn't it?" Astra turned to Hugo. "For us. If we could save a thousand."

He nodded.

"I plan to start next week," said Kostas.

"I'll give you a hand on weekends," Hugo offered, "once the exams are over."

Kostas protested, saying that Hugo had enough of building work during the week at the construction site.

"This would be different."

"I could help, too," said Astra. "Why not? I'm fit and strong. Just give me the chance to mix concrete! And, Kostas, you can help me when we buy *our* plot!"

Irena thought buying a plot of land a foolish idea. She and Hugo had made up again after a day when she had not spoken to him.

"You don't know anything about wiring and plumbing or things like that."

"We can learn. And Kostas' street is full of immigrants all helping one another. Some are electricians and plumbers."

Tomas thought the idea brilliant until he realized that they would not be able to buy a plot of land in the neighborhood they were now in. They'd have to go out to the suburbs, to the edge of the city.

"I don't want to leave my friends!"

"It would be ages before we'd have the house actually built, Tom," said Astra. "You'd be in high school by then, and you could probably still go to the same school as Sandy and Don."

Kristina and Lukas were less excited by the news. "A piece of land that will first have to be cleared and bull-dozed? And then we would have to build a house with our own hands?" asked Lukas.

"*Our* hands, Father," said Astra.

"But what can you children know about house building?"

156

There was a time when Lukas would not have balked at the idea. But he was older now, had less energy, and of course there could be no question of either him or their mother doing any physical work on the house.

"And don't you think you have enough to do with your jobs and your studying?"

"Kostas would help us," said Hugo. "I'm going to help him on Sundays."

"I will, too," put in Tomas. "Lots of my friends at school would help as well."

Hugo signaled to Astra and Tomas to back off. Their father's face was closed tight against the project.

"I think we should let the idea simmer for the present," he advised, when they had withdrawn. "But we can keep saving, and then we shall see."

Spring had given way to summer. Exam time arrived. Hugo and Astra were allowed to take a week's unpaid vacation from work. Irena was given time off from the library.

The twins enjoyed the week.

"Imagine not having to go to the cleaner's today!"

"I can't say I'll miss the construction site."

After the first papers their anxiety about being up to standard lessened. They became quietly confident. They always knew that they had been well taught. Many of their teachers had been university professors.

Between exams they went walking and explored other parts of the city. They took the streetcar along Queen Street and went to High Park. They lay on the grass, sunned themselves, and watched the black squirrels running up and down the trees.

"We don't get enough time to do this," said Astra. "I seldom seem to see you these days, Hugo."

"We're always working."

"Or you're with Irena."

Hugo was silent.

"What are you going to do about Bettina?"

"Stop asking me that!" He sat up, angry with her, but even more with himself, she saw.

"I don't *keep* asking. But perhaps you *should* break your engagement, Hugo."

"I couldn't possibly do that." Their parents had brought them up to be honorable, to keep their word once they had given it. "The Schneiders saved my life, Astra. I'm hoping that I can persuade Bettina to come over here."

"In that case, you really should not raise Irena's hopes."

"I know. I didn't really mean to—it just seemed to happen. I think I've got myself in a mess."

Astra touched him on the shoulder. He had taken off his glasses and was rubbing his eyes. She said softly, "I'm not trying to badger you. Truly."

"When the exams are over, I shall tell Irena."

They rose and dusted the grass from their clothes. They walked across to the pond and stood on the path, looking at the ducks and the Canada geese. Tomas loved drawing the geese, with their elegant black necks and heads and the white ruff around their throats.

Astra became suddenly aware of someone staring at her. She looked around. Drew Johnstone was standing farther along the path. For a moment their eyes connected, then Astra turned back to Hugo.

"Someone you know?"

"No, not really."

Hugo kept to his resolution. He explained to Irena that they must not see each other alone any more. He was apologetic. She was distressed. He was miserable. She wept. He looked on helplessly. She said she loved him. He did not know what to say. She rushed off to her mother to be comforted.

Thereafter, Mrs. Simmonds looked at Hugo with reproach, and he did not blame her. He was unable to look her in the eye. She was cool toward all the Petersons. Irena spoke only to Lukas and to Tomas. She seemed to think that Astra and Kristina had been against her. Tensions built up in the house, as did the heat under the roof, where the young Petersons found it almost impossible to sleep at night.

The twenty-third of June—John's Day—is a very special day for Latvians. They gather on its eve, to eat, drink, sing, and celebrate the summer solstice.

"Will we have our John's Day here?" asked Tomas.

"We can't light a bonfire in Mrs. Simmonds' backyard," said Astra.

"It's not fair! We must have a bonfire."

The custom was for the children to jump over the bonfire—that was the part that Tomas liked best.

It began to look as if they might not be able to have a celebration, and then some people at church asked them to join theirs. About thirty people gathered. A huge bonfire was lit—over which the children were not permitted to jump until it had almost died down—and they all stood around singing songs of Latvia. The girls braided bands of flowers to encircle their heads. There was beer and lemonade to drink, and slices of a special cheese, thick with caraway seeds, to eat.

Last year, Astra thought, we were in Esslingen. No, don't think of last year! This was this year, they were in Toronto, the evening was fine, and the sound of Latvian voices singing was filling the air.

On the last day of school, Tomas threw down his bike in the yard and came rushing into the kitchen, where Astra and Kristina were cooking supper. He had something under his arm.

"Guess what?" He was jumping up and down.

"Old Whacky's given you a raise?" said Astra.

"I won the art prize at school! I got a box brownie." He took the camera from its box to show to them.

"That's wonderful, Tom!" Kristina gave him a hug.

After supper, they all lined up on the porch and had their photograph taken. Tomas did not rush; he made sure they were properly grouped and that the sun was in the right place. He eyed them through the viewfinder.

"Okay everyone, smile!"

Click! The picture was taken. Forever afterward, Tomas would remember the end of his first Canadian school year.

He felt less happy the next day. He had committed himself to working six full days a week for the summer, and recently Mr. Zawacki had been giving him a harder and harder time. Also, the carrier was jiggling about because the welding had come loose and Mr. Zawacki had repaired it with a bit of wire. Tomas had asked him if he thought that was a good idea. Maybe it would be better to get it fixed properly? The grocer, in return, had demanded, "What do you think I am—made of money?"

That afternoon the temperature soared into the upper nineties, and humidity was high. By four o'clock Tomas thought he was going to melt and that nothing would be left of him but a pool of sticky liquid on the road.

He came back into the store for his last load.

"And then afterwards I want you to hose down the yard. In this weather we must keep everything fresh."

"Everything but me."

"What you say?"

"Nothing."

Tomas pushed the heavily laden bike out into the street and threw his leg over the bar. As his right foot reached the pedal, the carrier lurched sideways. Tomas tried to save it. And then everything—carrier, contents, bike, Tomas—went spiraling onto the road.

Mr. Zawacki came panting out of the store. "What are you doing, you young fool? Look at the mess—all the sugar, eggs, *everything* ruined! *Ruined!* I take all this from your pay."

Tomas scrambled to his feet. "I told you it would come off."

"It is not the carrier—it is you! You do not keep your mind on your work. I think I may fire you."

"You can keep your stupid job," Tomas yelled and walked away, leaving the mess on the roadway.

The next day, he got a job on a construction site as a bricklayer's helper. It was a small site, only three men. Tomas told the foreman he was fourteen, nearly fifteen. He was tall for his age. He didn't think he'd fooled the foreman, but the man agreed to take him on anyway, at a lower rate. The work was harder than delivering groceries, but he was earning twice as much. As he sweated under the broiling heat of the July sun, he kept his mind fixed on a gleaming chrome bicycle with whitewall tires. Maybe he should be giving all of his money toward their house, but he wanted the bicycle so much he was prepared to live in a tent!

It was hot in the dry cleaner's, too, even with all the windows open and the ceiling fan going. The women complained. Their feet swelled, and their nylon overalls clung to their backs. Gloria forsook her high heels and shuffled about in canvas sneakers. Nancy said it was just as well she had the thought of Saturday nights to keep her going.

She came in one Monday morning singing "For Every Man There's a Woman." She twirled about, letting her skirt fly out from the waist.

"You met a boy?" said Astra.

"Yeah, I did. U of T Medicine. He was there with his friend. Guess who his friend was? Somebody you know!"

"Nancy, I'm not interested."

"He's interested in you."

"Too bad!"

"Hey, listen!" Nancy grabbed her by the arm. "He explained to me why he didn't phone you."

"It would have to be a very good explanation."

"Don't be so proud!"

"Why shouldn't I be?"

"Look, Astra, he was going with this girl, see? The one in the pink skirt. And on the day before he met you they'd had a fight. She'd told him to drop dead. So he came to the Pier. He liked you and he wanted to call you, but the very next morning she came around to see him and said she was sorry, she hadn't meant it, blah-blah. So they made up again for a while. But now they're finished for good, and he'd like to see you again. So what do you say?"

"If he was here, I'd probably tell him to drop dead, too!"

A week after starting as a bricklayer's helper, Tomas passed out from the heat. The foreman drove him home in his car. Lukas exploded.

162

"You have been employing my son full-time on your site? He is not yet thirteen years old! This is exploitation!"

"Lay off, Father," pleaded Tomas weakly.

"You sit down and stay out of this! You look like death."

"Now see here, Mr. Petersons. He told me he was nearly fifteen—"

"And you were fool enough to believe him? Come on, you can see he is only a kid. You were able to pay him less money."

"You must have known he was working."

"He said he was just doing odd jobs around a site, but not *eight* hours a day in this terrible sun! What if he has sunstroke? If I have to call a doctor, how do I pay him?"

Tomas chipped in, "You owe me a week's wages, Mr. Jack."

The foreman put thirty dollars on the table. "That's nearly double," he said. Bike money, thought Tomas, feeling suddenly better.

He was forbidden to take on any such jobs again. "You must ask me first and tell me the truth about it, understand?" said Lukas.

Tomas was made to lie on the downstairs couch for the following day with the blinds drawn, but the next morning he went downtown and bought his bicycle. He was so excited he couldn't eat any breakfast.

The full price of the bike was sixty-two dollars and fifty cents, but the paint was a bit scuffed on the cross-bar, so the man had agreed to knock off seven fifty. Tomas had fifteen dollars saved, there was the thirty from the foreman, and the family had agreed to lend him ten. His father had said they couldn't be expected to sweat and save *all* the time. It was good for the soul to get its

163

heart's desire sometimes. It was essential. Or else you might lose heart altogether.

"And, Tom, I remember what it's like to be twelve years old and want something badly!"

For three days Tomas had perfect freedom, went cycling with Sandy and Don and swimming in Lake Ontario. Then Mr. Zawacki came around to apologize and ask if he'd like his old job back.

"Maybe I been a bit hasty. It was very hot day, not good for tempers."

Tomas hesitated. He couldn't spend the rest of the summer goofing around, not earning anything, and he and Mr. Zawacki got on all right on the whole, even though they scrapped a bit.

"Okay," he agreed, "but for five hours a day only. And I want a raise. Another five cents an hour."

Mr. Zawacki groaned. "You drive a hard bargain, boy! What can I do?" He threw up his hands. "Start tomorrow." He looked back. "And don't be late!"

Hugo walked home, thinking of cool water running down his face and back. His clothes were stuck to him with dust and sweat. July might have been bad, but if anything, August was proving to be worse. Kostas and he had been talking that day about looking for other jobs. Now that their English was improving, they felt they might have some chance of white collar employment.

"Perhaps you could get a job in a bank, Hugo, or a laboratory now that you have passed your courses." Hugo and Astra had passed all their exams. The family had had a big celebration, with special food and wine, and Kostas had joined them. He was thinking that next year he would take some classes himself. He had given up any idea of being able to practice law again. To re-

164

train here would take too long—five years—and he would not be able to afford it.

Hugo sat down on the porch steps to ease off his boots. He pulled off his socks. What a stink! Almost as bad as the skunk's. He took off his glasses and wiped his forehead with the back of his arm. Once they had reached their target of a thousand dollars, he would try to find other employment, even if it paid a little less than the site.

The screen door opened at his back, and his mother came out onto the porch.

"What's happened?" he asked quickly, for he knew by her face that something had.

"It's Frau Schneider, Hugo. She died this morning, very suddenly. A telegram came an hour ago."

Hugo could not take it in. Frau Schneider was *dead?* Only yesterday he'd had a letter from Bettina telling him they had all been at the inn for supper and her parents had been dancing as much as any of the young people. Her mother had been feeling much better. She must have had a relapse. And of course, letters took at least two weeks to come from Germany. In the interval between dispatch and receipt much could happen.

Hugo shook his head, trying to clear it. Kristina sat down on the step beside him and slipped her arm through his.

"I know you were very fond of Frau Schneider."

He nodded. She had been like a second mother to him. His throat felt as though it might burst if he were to speak. He swallowed, then he said, "I ought to go to Bettina."

TWELVE

I REALLY *ought* to go,'' Hugo said again.

Bettina and her father would be pleased if he were to come. He would be able to help them through a difficult and painful time. He would be like a son to Herr Schneider. But how could he pay his fare across the Atlantic without taking money from their home fund? He would have to ask his family to make a considerable sacrifice. He shook his head.

"It's out of the question."

"I rather think it is, Hugo," said Kristina slowly. "To go by boat would take a long time—you would arrive after the funeral. And I believe that to fly costs a great deal of money." The kind of people that they came across were not well enough off to travel by air. Some said that in years to come it would be the only way to travel; no one would take time to go by ship. "I am sure that neither Bettina nor her father will expect you to come. Not for the funeral, anyway. Perhaps later? That is something you will have to decide for yourself."

They spoke no more of the matter; this was not the time for it.

Thoughts raced through Hugo's mind. Now Bettina would not be able to leave her father. She was his only child, she was devoted to him, and his health was not good. As long as he was alive, she would not come to Canada.

The next morning he went to the telegraph office as soon as it opened and sent a telegram. "Deeply sorry. Unable to come to funeral. Writing. Fondest love to both, Hugo." He dictated the message in German, spelling out each word.

When he sat down in the evening to write the letter, he found it hard to know what to say, apart from how sorry and how grieved he was. They looked so paltry, those few lines on the paper, so inadequate. He wished that he could speak to Bettina, even for a few minutes, but the Schneiders did not have a telephone.

He had to wait more than two weeks before a reply came back. "We are very sad," Bettina wrote. "It is like having a great big hole in our house. I am worried for Father, though he is brave, as you would imagine. But he is alone so much of the time, when I am away at the hospital.

"We understood that you could not come. It is a very long and a very expensive journey. I cannot begin to imagine what North America is like. It is so far away, and everything seems so big compared to here."

Labour Day—a holiday marking the end of the summer vacation—came around. The intense heat had passed; it was now September. The space under the Simmonds' roof became bearable at night again.

The Petersons decided to take a picnic and go to Centre Island. They invited Kostas to join them. Hugo often brought him home to eat with them on Sunday evenings. He had come to be like part of the family. He had no family of his own in Canada and only a cousin or two surviving back in Lithuania. Hugo told him it would do him good to take a day off, and he agreed.

"What is it that they say about all work and no play?"

"Makes Kostas a dull boy!"

"I must not let that happen."

They crossed to the island on the ferry. The citizens of Toronto were there in force, enjoying the holiday, sitting on the grass, eating and drinking, playing ball games. Tomas had brought a soccer ball, and he badgered Hugo, Kostas, and Astra until they got up and played with him. Later in the day, he met up with some other boys his own age and organized a game with them. As Kristina said, he made friends easily.

She had made chicken salad sandwiches for the picnic and *pīragīs*—with chopped egg, as well as bacon and onions—and lemon cheesecake. And she had bought a delicious coffee and walnut cake from a Yugoslav baker.

"A good feast for a holiday," commented Lukas. "It is not often these days that we do something together as a family." He smiled as he reclined on one elbow and surveyed the other picnickers. His face had fleshed out a little and recovered much of its color. He had spent most of the summer sitting under the trees in the backyard reading and working. "You all have your own interests, and that is how it should be."

"It is good to have you with us, too, Kostas," said Kristina.

"Indeed." Lukas nodded.

"I am very happy to be here with you."

They stayed longer than they had intended. The ferry and streetcar going home were thronged. Lukas was in a good mood and did not complain about the crowds.

"Our first Labour Day!" said Tomas.

He went back to school the next day, happy to go. He would rather be at school than working five hours a day for Mr. Zawacki. Who wouldn't? And he couldn't wait to get back on the basketball court.

There were two new boys in their class. Claudio was from Milan, in Italy, and Leo from Kiev, in the Ukraine. They stood one on either side of the principal, looking at the floor.

"Tom!" Mr. Phillips beckoned to him. "You come and look after Leo for me, will you?"

Tomas got up and went to the front, feeling a little bit important. Well, yes, he did. He felt as if he belonged now. He was not a new boy any longer, he knew the ropes.

"Leo speaks very little English, but I am sure you can help him."

"Yes, sir."

Tomas took Leo back to his seat. Sandy had to move out of the desk next to Tomas so that the new boy could have it. He was not so pleased about that and gave Tomas a cross look as if it were his fault.

"Sandy," said Mr. Phillips, "you can look after Claudio and sit over here. You will have to help him with his English, too."

At recess there seemed to be a number of new pupils in the yard. Snatches of many different languages could be heard.

"They're letting way too many foreigners in, that's what my dad says," said Walter, a boy in Tomas's class. "It's okay, Tom! I didn't mean *you!* But before long they're going to swamp us—that's what my dad says, anyway."

* * *

169

Students began to appear again around the university. Astra refused to walk up University Avenue with Nancy.

"Absolutely not!"

"If you don't care about him, what are you worrying about? We might meet someone else."

"I can hardly remember what he looks like!"

Nancy sighed. She had not taken offense—she never did.

"Come on, girls, back to work!" called Gloria.

Astra returned to her trouser press to think about evening class. She planned to take four this year. Lukas thought that would be too much, but Hugo had promised to help her with algebra, and Lukas himself could coach her in Latin. She could not afford to spread the classes over too many years, or she'd be an old woman by the time she got to the university.

"Hey, *Astra!*"

She looked up. Nancy was signaling to her from around the corner.

"Someone to see you," she whispered.

Astra felt suddenly anxious. Was something wrong at home? Why else would someone come for her at work? They were always apprehensive about Lukas, even though he was looking much better. He was still on daily medication, would be for the rest of his life. The bills were a drain on the family budget, but they could cope. She hurried through to the front. She was not supposed to leave her place, but Gloria could only bawl her out, and they all knew that her bark was a lot worse than her bite.

Standing in front of the counter was Drew Johnstone.

"You!" she exclaimed. She was furious with him for coming to see her here, coming to see her dressed like this! She had on her oldest clothes, her face was hot, and her hair was a mess. And she was furious, too, with Nancy, who was nowhere to be seen.

"How would you like to go to the movies with me tonight?"

"Astra!" She heard Gloria's voice in the background.

"I'd like you to come."

Gloria's voice was getting louder. Nancy came sidling back in to stand demurely behind the counter.

Gloria now appeared. "What are you doing here, Astra? You know you're not allowed through the front—" She broke off when she saw Drew, and her voice changed. "Can I help you, sir?"

Sheepishly he produced a jacket and said that he'd brought it in for cleaning.

"Nancy here will attend to you. Back to work now, Astra, if you please!" Gloria spoke sweetly, giving Astra a scowl as she turned.

"Just a minute, Astra!" Drew grabbed her hand across the counter. "Please come! *Please!*"

"Oh—all right!"

"Call for you at seven."

Astra went back to the trouser press, followed by Gloria, tapping along on her high heels.

"You know I don't like boyfriends calling here!"

"He's not a boyfriend," said Astra, and brought down the top board to release a hiss of steam.

In the end they never did make it to the movies. When Drew called for her, Kristina opened the door and invited him in. Lukas then engaged him in conversation about his forefathers, who had come to Canada in the early nineteenth century among the earliest pioneers. His great-great-grandmother had cleared the bush single-handed, from the sounds of it. Bully for her! thought

Astra. She had been one of those amazing women who could build log houses alongside the men, raise eight children, bury another half dozen, sew quilts, break the ice on the water pail in the mornings when the temperature had dropped to twenty below, bake bread, make quince jelly, and have time left over in the evenings to write a book about it all.

After the saga of Drew's family history (which Astra found herself listening to with some interest), he and Hugo got to talking about medicine and the medical faculty at the University of Toronto. And when they did finally get up to go, Tomas escorted them out so that he could have a good look at Drew's Ford convertible.

While he and Drew had their heads under the hood and Astra was standing on the sidewalk, Irena came along. They nodded to each other. They spoke very little nowadays. Kristina had said that she thought it would be good if Astra could try to heal the breach, but she didn't know where to start, what to say. The atmosphere in the house was strained, and the Petersons felt that their time for staying with the Simmonds was running out.

"I like your family," said Drew, as they drove off.

"I am glad," she said sarcastically.

He laughed. "You *are* stubborn, aren't you!"

They went to a drugstore and drank coffee. He repeated the story about the girlfriend.

"I know—Nancy told me all that."

"But you don't believe me?"

She raised one shoulder, as much as to say that she neither believed nor disbelieved. "I don't know you."

"Why don't you try to get to know me? Why don't you give me a chance?"

* * *

Tomas was riding his own bike back from the grocery store when he heard a bicycle bell ringing behind him and a voice calling "Hey, Tom! *Tom!*" A girl's voice. One that he recognized. He swerved.

She caught up with him.

"You just getting home from work? What's Mr. Zawacki like to work for? Mum says he's got an awful temper on him. She says he has tantrums sometimes."

"He's all right," said Tomas gruffly. He was not going to discuss Old Whacky with *her!* Anyway, what a nerve *she* had asking him about his work.

"That's a great bike you've got. I like whitewall tires. They're real cute."

Now she was trying to soft-soap him! *Cute,* for goodness sake! It was enough to make him want to get rid of them. He said, "I want to ask you something. Why did you tell Miss Lawson about me working? Sandy said he told *you.*"

"It wasn't me that told!" Now she swerved and almost ran into his front wheel. She was bristling with indignation. "Cross my heart it wasn't."

"Who else could it have been?"

"*Everybody* knows you work for Old Whacky. Always have. Course they do! They see you, don't they, on the grocer's bike? They'd need to be blind not to."

Tomas could not argue with that. Maybe it was Alice Jones who had told. He had a feeling it might have been. But what did it matter? It had all happened ages ago—light years, it seemed.

"I'm sorry," he muttered.

"That's okay. I'm having a party Saturday night. Seven o'clock. I'll be asking Sandy and Don and everybody. Would you like to come?"

"Yeah, all right. Thanks."

173

"See you then!"

"See you, Carol!"

The foundations of Kostas' house were down, the basement walls had reached ground level. He wanted to get the floor and tar paper on before the onset of winter, though he thought he would probably wait until spring before he moved in. Then he would give up his caretaking job.

"You could take it over, Hugo. There are three rooms in my apartment, just enough for your family perhaps?"

"We'd be able to manage, that's what we have at the moment."

"And you'd be able to save faster."

Hugo went most Sundays to lend a hand, and Astra occasionally. Now that she was seeing Drew regularly and studying again, she did not have much free time. Tomas went, though, and brought along Sandy and Don. The boys enjoyed lugging concrete blocks about and mixing mortar. They worked enthusiastically. Perhaps even a bit too enthusiastically at times, for Kostas' and Hugo's liking, when mortar flew a little high and had to be scraped off unsuitable places. But, on the whole, they were more of a help than a hindrance.

One Sunday, Drew's convertible pulled up in the road.

"I've brought Drew to see your piece of land, Kostas," said Astra. "His great-great-grandparents built their own house when they first came to Canada. Out of logs. After they'd trekked overland and felled the jungly, mosquito-infested forest. Think how lucky you are! You can get a bus at the end of the road."

Drew made a face at her. She liked to tease him about his ancestors.

They stayed a little while at the site, talking to Kostas and Hugo, then drove off again.

"Where to now?" she asked.

"I thought I might take you home for tea."

The Johnstones lived in a house overlooking High Park and Grenadier Pond. Its back sat high over the ravine. Astra felt herself go quiet as they pulled up outside it. The front lawn was as smooth and as green as a billiard table, and a shiny new Cadillac was parked in the driveway. When Drew had suggested bringing her home, she had protested, saying she wasn't sure if she wanted to.

"Why not?" he'd asked. "I know all your family."

"Too well!" Every time he called for her, he spent the first hour talking to them, unless she headed him off.

"Do they know I'm coming?"

"They're used to me bringing friends home."

"You didn't answer my question."

"Stop it! They're not going to eat you. After all, you've survived nasty Russians and nasty Germans, so surely you can survive my parents!" He opened her door. "And yes, I did tell them."

Mr. Johnstone was an older version of Drew, and Astra relaxed with him at once. Mrs. Johnstone she was less sure of. She was immaculately dressed in a fine tweed skirt, matching sweater set, and pearls; and she was very nice to the new visitor, seeing that she was comfortable, refilling her tea cup, offering chocolate fudge cake. Astra really could not fault her in any way.

She knew what the problem was, of course; one didn't have to be a psychologist to work that out. Mrs. Johnstone saw her as a threat. Drew was the only son—he had an older sister, married and gone—and he was in his second year at the university, with a long way to go before he'd be fully qualified. She could read his mother's thoughts. Far too young to be having a steady girlfriend. Far too young to think of settling down—

especially with a *DP* who works in a *dry cleaner's* for goodness sake! Astra wished she could say to Mrs. Johnstone, "Don't worry, I'm young, too, and I have a lot that *I* want to do. I don't intend to stay in a dry cleaner's all my life. And I'm not like my friend Mara in Boston, who's just got engaged. I'm not trying to settle down with your son. We just like being together, that's all." It was a pity one couldn't say what was on one's mind at times. She thought Mrs. Johnstone might upset her tea if she tried to.

Mr. Johnstone was very interested in Astra's family history. His brother had visited Riga once on business, when he was a young man.

"Fine city, I believe. What a shame for your family!"

"Do you think you'll ever go back?" inquired Mrs. Johnstone. She asked questions with the air of one who felt she ought to be asking something in order to be polite.

"Don't suppose you will, will you?" said her husband.

"Probably not. *We* realize that—Hugo, Tomas, and I—but our parents go on hoping."

"One can't blame them."

Drew's father and Astra talked so long that the smell of cooking chicken began to drift in from the kitchen.

"Why don't you stay for supper, Astra," Mr. Johnstone invited. He looked at his wife.

"Yes," she said, still polite. "Would you like to, Astra? Or does your family expect you back?"

Over supper, Mr. Johnstone said, "It's a waste for a girl like you to be working in a dry cleaner's. You're far too intelligent."

"I won't do it forever. I'm hoping to go to the university some day."

176

"You *are?*" Mrs. Johnstone sounded surprised. "Your family would be pleased."

A step up for us, I suppose is what she's thinking, thought Astra.

"Her father was a professor, Mother," put in Drew, "at the university in Riga. And her mother is an artist."

"Oh, really?"

"You know, Astra," said Mr. Johnstone, "I could use you in my law office, especially with your knowledge of languages. Why don't you come in and see me, and we could discuss it?"

Hugo, encouraged by Astra finding office work, set about looking for a different job for himself. Someone told him to go to the YMCA and ask their advice. They were helpful, gave him suggestions to follow up, and eventually he was offered a job as a technician in a university laboratory. He would be earning slightly less than on the building site.

"Take it!" said Lukas. "Money is not the only thing in this life. Never forget that! This year we have had to think about it so much that at times my head has been in danger of turning into a cash register."

Kostas, encouraged by Hugo's example, found a clerking job.

Hugo wrote to tell Bettina about the changes in their lives. He found that he did not have a great deal to tell. The daily comings and goings of their lives could not possibly interest her. Their letters to each other were getting shorter and shorter.

The parents of Tomas's friend Don invited the Petersons family to join them for Thanksgiving dinner.

177

"This is most kind of you, Mrs. Owen," said Lukas, presenting her with a bottle of wine.

"Most kind," said Kristina, who had brought rust and gold chrysanthemums. The colors of fall, thought Astra. The trees were ablaze with foliage, dazzling red, sizzling orange, and golden yellow. The days were shortening; there was a nip in the air. Another winter was on its way. At work, people were talking about getting out their winter coats, and those who had summer cottages on the lakes up north were planning to close them down this weekend.

"We're delighted you could come," said Mrs. Owen. "Since this is your first Thanksgiving in Canada, I thought you might like to have a typical Canadian Thanksgiving dinner."

They had roast turkey with cranberry sauce, all the other trimmings, and fruit pies to follow.

"You must try pumpkin pie," said Mrs. Owen, cutting it into large wedges.

"I warn you—you may not like it!" Mr. Owen laughed. "*I* don't. Give me good old apple or cherry any day."

The Petersons were not sure about pumpkin pie, either—it looked and tasted a bit like mashed turnip—but they ate it to the last crumb, even though Mrs. Owen told them to leave it if they didn't like it. They were still incapable of leaving anything on their plates.

"They say the squirrels have been harvesting a lot of nuts," said Mr. Owen, and explained. "That means it's going to be a hard winter! I'll need to get my wood chopped. You going to help me tomorrow, Don?"

"I guess."

"I like chopping wood," put in Tomas.

"You've got yourself a job!" said Mr. Owen.

The Petersons enjoyed the meal and their evening with

178

the Owens. It was a celebration that held no echoes of the past for them, unlike Christmas or Easter.

"You must come and visit us," said Kristina when they were leaving, "and we shall cook you a Latvian dinner."

On the day that Hugo finished at the building site, he sat down to write the most difficult letter that he had ever had to write.

"I must tell you what is on my mind, Bettina. I have been trying to look into the future and see what there is for us. And all that I can see are difficulties that seem insoluble.

"I know you would not leave your father, but I cannot abandon my family, either. If I did, Astra would have to carry the whole financial burden. We would like Mother to give up her cleaning job as soon as possible. She has gotten some work doing illustrations for greeting cards, which she loves, but it does not pay much, nor do Father's translating jobs. Tomas, too, earns only a little. We are struggling hard to save money for a home of our own. If I left, they could not manage it on their own.

"And Mrs. Simmonds has given us notice to go at the end of November. She says that she needs the rooms for her brother's family. We have found an apartment in a street nearby but, once more, it will be temporary. We cannot go on like this forever, moving from one place to the other."

And then he forced himself to set down the most difficult part of all—that he felt that he had no alternative but to break off their engagement.

His letter crossed with Bettina's.

"I am writing to ask you to release me from our betrothal, Hugo. I have been thinking about this for some time. It would be too many years before we could ever think of marrying. You are making a new life out there in Canada, and mine is here, in the village, with my father and the people I have known since I was born.

"Do you remember Hans, Hilde's cousin? He works on the railway—like Father. We have become fond of each other, and I think it is very likely that one day we may marry . . ."

The last sentence pierced him unexpectedly sharply. Bettina was thinking of marrying someone else! It was only now that he was beginning to realize fully what the break would mean. It would be final. He might never see Bettina again. He pushed up his glasses and pressed his fingertips against his hot eyelids. For a moment he sat slumped forward over his desk; then he got up and went to find his mother.

She was in the kitchen ironing. The smell of the warm clothes took him back to the Schneiders' kitchen, and he wanted to go there, now, and see Bettina. The desire was like an ache in his chest. He thrust the letter into Kristina's hand. She read it quickly, then looked up at him.

"I still feel attached to her, Mother. I feel I'm losing something important out of my life."

"You're bound to be upset," Kristina said gently. "And I'm sure she will be, too. I'm afraid, dear, that you're victims of time and circumstance. But you're young, both of you. I know that when you *are* young, you get fed up hearing that! But the hurt *will* lessen—believe me."

She passed the letter back. At the end Bettina had written, "I shall never forget you, Hugo."

* * *

Weekly, Astra and Hugo had been going to the bank to make a deposit in their home fund. They met on Fridays, at lunchtime, to do it. As the days grew shorter, their balance grew bigger.

And then came the day when the figures in the bank book read $1,000.

"We've made it!" Astra cried and threw her arms around Hugo, almost knocking off his glasses.

"Mind my glasses! I can't afford any new ones now. We'll need all the money we can lay our hands on."

They went to a restaurant to have a celebratory lunch and discuss tactics. They had already picked out a plot in Willowdale, not far from Kostas', and had indicated their interest to the seller. The price was six hundred and eighty dollars, which would leave something over for initial expenses.

All that remained now was to convince their parents.

Lukas was incensed by a report from Moscow in the newspaper. It was the thirty-second anniversary of the Russian revolution, and Georgi Malenkov, who was Deputy Chairman of the Council of Deputies, had made a speech saying that the peoples of the Soviet Union were more closely united today than ever before.

" 'Never has our country had such just and well-ordered frontiers as now,' " Lukas read aloud. "Lies! All lies! *Just* boundaries? When our people are prisoners and cannot leave? Unable to come and go, unable even to speak their minds?"

"Calm down, Father." Astra laid a hand on his arm. "We know it's lies. But don't forget your blood pressure. Don't let Malenkov put that up!"

"You're right." Lukas folded the paper and put it away.

The twins looked at each other. Then Hugo said, "We want to talk to you—about a plot of land."

When they had finished talking, Lukas said, "Five hundred of those dollars are not ours, don't forget. They are only on loan."

"We can pay them back later," said Hugo.

"I don't like all this paying back later! We would have to find money to build the house, money to live. I do not want to be in debt. I have never been in debt in my life—never until now. I have always taken great care not to be."

"That was before the war," said Astra. "In Latvia. Father, this is a different world. We've got the chance to buy a piece of land. We could build our own house on it. Then we could do what *we* want. No one could put us out. Mother?" Astra turned to her. "What do you think?"

"I'm torn. I see your father's point; I see yours and Hugo's too."

There was something else besides money bothering Kristina and Lukas, their children realized. If they were to go ahead and buy the land, they would be making a commitment. It would be tantamount to saying, "We will settle here. We accept that we shall not return to our own country. We concede victory to dictators like Stalin and Malenkov. *This* will be our country now."

"Houses can always be sold, Mother," said Hugo.

"Would it not be better to buy a house?" she suggested. "The way Mrs. Simmonds did, and take in boarders to help pay the mortgage?"

"That would be one way," Hugo admitted. "But the only house we could afford would be in a run-down area."

"And we'd have to have other people in it," said Astra. "It wouldn't just be *ours*. And the house would probably be pretty run-down, so we'd have to spend a lot of time fixing it up. Wouldn't it be better to start from scratch? On a new piece of land? Make a new beginning."

"And where do you think we'll find money for building materials when we have rent to pay at the same time?" Lukas demanded. "How can we go and live in a basement?"

"I'm taking over Kostas' caretaking job in the spring," said Hugo. "It's arranged. We'll be able to live rent free there for as long as we like. Until the whole house is finished, if we want to."

"You've *got* to come and see our land!" said Tomas.

"It's not *ours* yet," said Lukas sharply.

They went on Sunday. They took the streetcar and then the bus.

"Cows," observed Lukas, clearing a space on the fogged-up window to look out.

No one remained on the bus after they got off. They stood in the roadway watching its tail lights disappear. November rain was falling, cold and sleety.

"It's miles out," said Lukas, who was bundled up in his tweed overcoat, hat, and scarf. "Miles from the library. Miles for you all to travel to work."

"Other people do it," said Hugo. "And it's not *that* far. They say the city will spread out miles farther yet. They say the population will double, even triple in size."

The road leading to their plot was as yet unpaved. It had been raining heavily during the week, and the path was like a muddy quagmire. Hugo took his father's arm to help keep him from slipping. He pointed out that the sewers were soon to be dug and the water supply laid

183

in. They were not proposing to buy an unserviced lot. Some people, who lived even farther out, did, and had to put in their own septic tanks. Lukas made no comment.

Astra held the big colored umbrella, borrowed from Drew, over Kristina's head. They should have waited until spring, she thought, when the weather was mild and the days lengthening. Why did they always seem to be doing things in November? It was a fateful month for them. They'd landed in Canada this time last year; they'd arrived in German-occupied Poland as refugees in November 1944.

In spite of the weather, several people were working on their sites. They looked wet and bedraggled. A building site on a wet day was not an encouraging prospect. It made you want to be sitting in front of a fire in a finished, furnished room, with the curtains drawn.

They passed a basement roofed over with black tar paper. There was a light in the window.

"People are living in *there?*" asked Lukas. "It looks like a war bunker."

"Damp, I should think," said Kristina, shivering, pulling up her collar.

They reached the plot.

"Ah, a piece of woodland," commented Lukas.

"The trees can be felled," said Hugo.

"But we'd keep some at the back," said Astra, talking rather fast, feeling anxious. "They'd look pretty, and they'd make a shelter for the garden."

"It's wider than it looks," said Hugo.

"It's wide enough for a house," said Tomas.

'Is it?" Kristina smiled at him. He had shot up in the last year. He was thirteen, and stood level with her, now. "Of course, you are going to be our architect, aren't you, Tom?"

184

"I've made a plan." He pulled a crumpled sheet of paper from his pocket. "It may not be *exactly* right, but it'll give you an idea. I reckon we can have a living room, a small dining room, a kitchen, a bathroom, one decent-sized bedroom, and three little ones." He was determined to have a room of his own. Hugo was always studying, and grumbled if he even put the radio on low. He liked to listen to sports reports, Western music, and comedians like Amos 'n Andy.

Huddled under the red- and yellow-striped umbrella, they bent their heads over Tomas's plan.

"This is the living room," he said, pointing. "At the back. So that we can have a big window looking out to the woods."

"You seem to have thought of everything, Tom!" said his father.

They straightened their backs. All eyes were on Lukas.

"By spring we'll have saved enough money to build the basement," said Hugo. "We'll have three hundred left after we've bought. *If* we buy, that is, of course. And once the basement is in, we can get a mortgage to do the rest. Kostas has just gotten one. And he's bought an old pickup truck for bringing in materials to the site. He says we can have the use of it too."

"It'll be cheaper in the long run to build than to buy an old house and remodel it," said Astra.

Rain drummed on the roof of the umbrella. They waited.

Astra thought of their old house in the country, back in Latvia, with its long verandah and wide, green lawn fringed with birch trees . . . She blinked. For a moment she had been there, sitting on the old rocking chair on the verandah; she could have sworn she'd heard the sharp trilling of the birds and the lowing of Klavins' cows from the meadow beyond. There'd been such peace, such *space*. Were her parents thinking of their old home, too? Such thoughts must be put away, however, like old photographs that can be brought out, to be looked at from time to time, but not dwelled on.

At length Lukas spoke.

"Do you children *really* think you can build a house? Aren't you being overoptimistic?"

They shook their heads.

"Well, well! It seems like the three of you have already made the decision. It would not be for old stick-in-the-muds like us to stop you. You've worked for the money and saved it, after all. I expect it will be a very fine house. What do you say, Kristina?"

"I expect so, too, Lukas. Very fine." She smiled. "One that I shall be happy to live in."

Then she slipped her arm through his, and with him carrying the umbrella aloft, they set off back down the path to the main road. The three younger members of the family stayed behind for a moment to gloat over their land.

"Imagine—*our* land!" said Astra, laughing, as rain ran down her face.

"It will really be *ours*?" asked Tomas.

"It really will," said Hugo. "Our very own."